RUBY LEAVING TEXAS

DALE LOTRECK

This is a work of fiction. Names, characters,
businesses, places, events and incidents are
either the product of the author's imagination
or used in a fictitious manner.
Any resemblance to actual persons, living or
dead, or actual events is purely coincidental.

RUBY LEAVING TEXAS

Ruby was the leavinest gal I ever knew. Ruby was a shining diamond in the night. Me, I had been in New York eight years and was ready to explode.

I rolled into the Cafe that New Year's Eve half-loaded and dosed for the first time in years. Last time I dropped, me and Johnny D ripped into town amid a kaleidoscope of intense fusion. 4th of July probably '82, we decided to dose in New York and see what the big thing was all about. Johnny, he'd been there done that, but me, I'd never ventured that far into the depths of the unknown. Born and raised in Connecticut, we didn't take no chances and life was linear...beginning, middle and end. Me, I guess I had fear. Hell, fear of this, fear of that, claustrophobia around that many people, but as the weight lifters say, "That which doesn't kill me, will make me stronger."

Somehow I was born into a middle class family in Connecticut, back when there was a middle class. I can't really say that the evaporation of that social class was a tragedy. The middle class was bottle-fed on the "Leave it to Beaver" ideals, and I always believed that problems could be resolved. We didn't have a teevee set until I was almost ten, so I can't say it was from that influence, but my brothers who are both younger are wholly dysfunctional with a teevee arrogant attitude that may be unsurpassed in this world. There are times when it is obvious that the Brady Bunch is halting all laws of Physics in their thirty-minute problem resolution before the next commercial. The real problem lies in the subliminal message that there can be problem resolution at all. Me, I went to say good-bye to Ruby with a loaded pistol and a spare clip. Just in case.

***

I moved to New York with $500 and a hard-on. I still have the hard-on, some things last longer than others.

I could go on about Connecticut, it's really not worth writing about. Perhaps one could just visualize the complete opposite about everything that goes down in New York and remember that the Puritans are still running things back in CT. It isn't so scary in the thick of it as it is on the outside, many years later, looking back in. Lack of comparison is what gives those Yankee elitists their smugness, and there's no one else but them.

In New York, people blow off so much steam all the time, that although they spend much of their lives in therapy, they are usually safe to be around. The Yankees that ended up in the Midwest somehow learned to keep a smiling face, maintain social order and then on their one fateful day go on down to that schoolyard with an AK47 and make the nightly news all around the globe.

"We never thought he would do this...he was such a good man and a good father. Fine church-going Christian, ya understand."

Me, I knew he would do it, hell they all will end up doing it and it would be a waste of time to analyze why. Look at the culture, look at the smiling faces. Hell, it's physically impossible to be that even all the time, and the factor is time...it's all a matter of time before our true colors rise to the surface, and Ruby...well Ruby, ol' gal, she's a chameleon. Ruby is such a colorful woman that sometimes you wish she'd find the one that suits her best and wear it proudly. But those colors, oh Lord those colors do change. Back in Connecticut, they don't let it out, they don't hold it in, the Walmarts are safe and your trust fund is about to mature. Fuck it, I'd rather live on the edge. We all are anyway and there's no sense living in that genetic denial and brag about how your people got off the Mayflower. They're dead now anyway so fuck it.

***

It's all life and death. You live and you die and everything in the middle is filler. Hell, it could be fantastic Cuban-seed, 12 year aged Bourbon filler and it could be pure manure, but that filler is what you add to it, the birth and death take care of themselves, the only thing we are responsible for is the filler, so it's not to waste any time. Time is the one thing you had yesterday that you ain't gonna have tomorrow. Not that same time, anyway, and people sit around and wait for something to happen.

Ruby was the only one I knew that could keep the same time. Her filler was good but good because it was raw and dramatic…it was also sad and it was tragic. Ruby, God bless her soul, had the saddest heart on Earth. I could see it in her eyes. Hell, I could just about reach out and touch it. She could sit there and tell you about her sadness, about her childhood and what went wrong. That poor darling was one of the most self-aware people I knew with one exception. Ruby said it couldn't be fixed. Things were the way things were and shit was shit. I suppose that the things that bring folks together ain't necessarily the things that keep folks together. I can't pinpoint exactly what brought us together. No matter how your mind twists and turns things, the first attraction is always physical. Man can build churches and preach and tell everyone how man is different, but the bottom line is Man is an animal who lives to eat and eats to fuck. It's so damned basic, but people wanna fuck things up and tell us how different we all are from the animals because we can make decisions and such, but can we really? It seems to me and always has, that the decisions are made far away from our consciousness, and we just walk right into trap after trap.

***

So there's Ruby coming in outa the cold on that lonely New Year's Eve 1990. Me, I'm glowing from the ingredients and play it cool as she sits down next to me, I try not to notice, I guess I got some female in me, sometimes defensive, definitely aloof. I don't like the way some men would embarrass themselves the way they do, just to get a little. Hell, I've gotten more than a little and I've never had to beg either. Perhaps I am slightly different from the rest of the animals. Perhaps it's predestined or perhaps I'm only kidding myself. So I'm cool until Slick, the bartender introduces us, but in a pre-calculated way trying to make him look like such the gentleman, which he never was anyway. Well I'm zooming light years a second so I don't really know if I'm a gentleman or not, but I do remember one thing. Last time I dosed, I loved New York so much I had to move there.

Me and Johnny D came down on that weekend, fireworks everywhere, zooming and we strolled on into Chinatown like a battle zone. Man, we were invincible. We tore on through that motherfucker without a scratch, without even a burn, two whiteboys from Connecticut. I guess unlike the Hippies and more like the Natives, I dosed for meaning and hell, I found it.

So Ruby sits there glowing in the darkness, an angel in the sea of night. Hell, if you met a girl in New York who wasn't out to rip you off, you were lucky. Ruby, however was different. Ruby was a good girl from a different time, and those eyes, Lord I loved her eyes.

***

Ruby, well Ruby believed in Karma, or so she said. Funny thing is right about now, I don't see Ruby and Karma seeing eye-to-eye. It's possible…maybe she's changed, or maybe she's adjusted her strict moral code to suit herself just a little bit better. Too much conflict can be stressful. I'm not saying she owes me anything, but that girl owes something somewhere. When we first met, Ruby preached about how her Daddy wasn't faithful and cheated on her Mother, and all men therefore were shit. Well me, I was gonna show Ruby just how faithful a man could be. I had been waiting for her my whole life. My whole life was full of faceless females, just important enough to lead me to her. It was time to leave the endless line behind, and I was gonna show Ruby just how good it could be.

So Ruby shined in the night. Ruby believed in right and wrong, and Ruby was gonna fight for the underdog. Her life had been bad enough and there was no one there to catch her whenever she fell, so she was gonna be there to catch all the falling angels she could save. Me, I was ready to move on, and I was going to go along for the ride. Ruby was the best gal I ever latched onto, her path was pure, and I was gonna help her help the world from itself. Ruby believed that what came around went around, perhaps it was her own sense of Justice. Just perhaps Ruby saw Karma as divine Justice and prayed to the Lord above, so those that hurt her were gonna get hurt themselves. Me, I was gonna help her. Damn it, for what they did to that sweet angel, I was gonna help make 'em pay. I loved that girl to death.

***

One night, up on my roof back on the Lower East Side, I used to hang out up there, chill out from those brutal New York days and look up at what stars there were, smoke a Newport and forget about things for a while. Used to be you could look over there across the street and see all those young Hippie chicks in their cribs, in that flop house turned "luxury apartments" with a new coat of paint, runnin' around naked and fucking their brains out, too poor to afford curtains, and too cool to care. The freak show was over, though. I just used to appreciate seeing people do what it is people do and forget what a bunch of assholes everyone was during the day.

***

Well anyway, I used to look over there, and not knowing who she was, I could feel her sadness. I used to look down on the street at the junkies gettin' shit beat out of 'em and told to wait 'cause that's what junkies do, they wait. I'd look up and down from one end to the other and see kids locked outside for a while 'cause their parents wanted to fuck in the one room apartment, and all those old enough not to care, drinking 40 oz bottles 'cause there was no place else to go, and for the first time, I laid my eyes on Ruby.

Not knowing who she was, I used to look across the street from up on my roof and see the blue gray glow of her teevee set giving her that company she never admitted she wanted. That poor girl used to sit there most of any given night watching the teevee alone, and later I found out she had a brother who lived right across the street. Well I saw the sad in her aloneness, I felt her pain and damn, after so many times, I swore I'd never feel another's pain, I felt hers, deep down in my gut.

Ruby had a sadness deep in her heart, Ruby poor gal, had demons. Ruby believed in Karma…Karma, I didn't realize then, was only one of Ruby's many colors.

***

Slick introduced us that fateful night and hell, I ain't been the same since. Perhaps how much I disliked Slick, I should let him have her, but in spite of what she did to me, she was and still is, too good for him. I knew that then. Ruby and me started making a connection, and it was good. Slick, the asshole, left his place behind the bar, took her from the barstool next to mine, and went out and danced around the dance floor with her. Slick, the asshole, just wouldn't let her go. Me, I'm a hero sonofabitch, and my problem resolution fantasy comes from years watching Randolph Scott and Humphrey Bogart doin' the right thing. Hell, Slick's way out of his league, Ruby needs rescuing, and me, I'm gonna save the day.

Slick used to play it like he was some martial arts badass. Slick, like every other undiscovered asshole on the block, used to make it like he was some big shit. Slick used to like to talk about all these big projects he had on the burner, but if anyone else was close enough to hear, Slick would up and say, *"but I don't want people around here to know what I'm working on!"* That would raise people's ears and his smug silence fed their imagination, and that does funny things to the mind. A great deal of a whole lotta people thought Slick was some kinda hot shit. To me, Slick was just some kinda shit without the heat.

Well, anyway, I'm sick of seeing Slick all over this stuff that's too good to be his and me being Randolph Scott and all, decides to step on in. I didn't ask could I cut in, I didn't see any necessity in being polite. I just strutted up, nice and slow, tap him on the back, and point over my shoulder, with my thumb, back to the bar where he belonged. Slick stopped and put his chest out like a rooster, but quickly realized I wasn't one of the sheepish wanna-be's he liked to surround himself with. I saw right through him. Eyeball-to-eyeball, he knew what was about to happen and he backed down quick. His bubble burst, mine inflated, and Ruby, sweet Ruby smiled like her knight had finally arrived. It happens in storybooks, it happened on the Lower East Side.

***

Ruby, she came to me in a dream. It was never predestined, I may not have ever dreamed about her in my life. I dream when I'm awake. I have visions that tell me where to go and what to do. I hear voices and I see the animals. I play out whole scenarios somewhere in between sleep and awake, and there's a lesson, always a lesson to be learned. There's not much difference between sleep and awake if you're really paying attention.

Ruby, she came to me in that dream I dreamt when I was awake. I was there looking right at her, knowing it was right, feeling her happiness, and not even knowing yet that I had already felt her pain. She is shining all over that sonofabitch Lower East Side, and Lord is she different. She carries a style and a grace from another age. She is dressed to kill in that green satin dress. She doesn't care what no other body thinks, and she is not hip and and she is not trendy, but there she is, standing high on the clouds, light years from anyone else. Ruby is from a place people don't know, and people haven't seen. Ruby is from a place I can't even describe. In the middle of all this, all this trendy New York androgyny, this casual dope use, this fuck-or-be-fucked reality of life on the Edge, Ruby glows with a presence, a steadfastness that this sonofabitch ghetto ain't ever seen. Goddamn I'm in love, and I didn't want it, I don't deserve it, and sure as shit I ain't ready for it, but from that very moment I met her, things sure did change.

Me, I can't even count the number I had the year before. It was no big deal, except I probably woulda gone insane without it. It was a little past the dawn of the Plague, and I was starting to be careful. It was ironic how only a few years prior, an experienced woman could roll you over into the depths of ecstasy and all of a sudden, almost overnight, "promiscuous" had become one of the warning signs of the Plague. Me, I needed companionship, and I sure didn't need any commitment. It became a sea of faceless bodies, willing but uncaring, but all any man really needed.

***

I had a few offers that New Year's Eve. I didn't take any of 'em too seriously, sometimes I think I may think too much. To me, they were only offers of mutual pity, and by now I was starting to feel that being alone was probably better than waking up miserable. Sometimes I like to think that I may be the one guy who wouldn't crawl through the dirt just because the blood is now in the other head. Sometimes I like to think I'm that different. Sometimes I wonder if anyone is really that different from anyone else.

So Ruby and me danced all night, she was having the time of her life. Me, I felt like I was some kid again, and I was dancing with this girl from another time, from another place, and damn, my feet were moving, the room was moving. Ruby showed me a good time, as I did her. It was like a second chance on everything else that had ever gone wrong and never would happen again.

Time was passing and I wanted to take her away from all this, from this place where everyone knew everyone else, where no one act would ever be forgotten. Ruby, she was in another world, and later told me she had five cordials before she got up the nerve to come down to the bar alone, that she had never been much of a social person, but that night she was a cat on fire. Before I could ask her to come outside, and upstairs with me, she planted a kiss on me, the like of which I have never felt. We melted in each other's arms. I'm not much for public displays, but lost all sense of time and place. I think we were still standing somewhere inside the bar. My head was swimming in her love. I lost time and I lost place, and that gorgeous woman took me where I've never been before. I couldn't wait to get her the hell out of there.

After much coaxing, we went up on my roof in its Full Moon glory. That New Year's Eve was like none before, and none after. The Lower East Side sky glowed in the Lunar Sun that bounced off her dark, auburn hair, and me an' Ruby danced beneath its magic. Sometime into the magic, we went downstairs and slowly spent the rest of the night, making up for lost time, catching up with past lives, and Lord did we connect…

***

Ruby, first sign of danger, turns and runs. I guess I figured me to be some kinda Superman hero gonna save her from all that fear. Hell, they're women, they run, they all run. They raise the young, they keep the nest…ain't a woman I've known been able to keep those defenses down very long. I'm probably lucky I had the girl as long as I did. Before too long, those bristles get up and in the way.

Well, me an' Ruby were lying there, arm in arm, basking in the aftermath, a single candle still flickering, danced off her ivory face. This is perhaps the first time New York has made sense to me. We are serene in our Holiness, we are just shaking in the beauty of it all, and all of a sudden, Ruby's got to go. Shit, it's five in the morning and it's cold outside, and why the hell would anyone wanna go all the way back across the street, and back up those stairs alone? I'm only gonna come over and get you again, Ruby. Well no, the party's over and Ruby's got to go back home. Well I can't make her decision for her, but I tell her that she's coming back in the morning for some breakfast. Well anyway, *so give me your number and I'm gonna wake you up first thing, and cook for you, sweet darling* and Ruby left in the early hours of the day's first light. That was the first time Ruby left.

***

Ruby had a daughter, Elizabeth, who was thirteen years old back then. Ruby was looking for something. Ruby had visited New York some time before that and ran around with her brother and some friends and thought this might be the something she was looking for.

Ruby, she never had a childhood, she had to be an adult when her folks couldn't be. Ruby raised her daughter and her blind brother when there was no one around to help. That poor girl had more shit than any one person should have to deal with. Ruby needed a break. Ruby had worked hard her whole life and Ruby had spent her energy making everyone else's life better, but with no time for herself. Ruby was ready for a vacation.

Elizabeth's father did not seem like a bad sort. I never met him, but spoke with him on the phone a few times. Ruby always called him an asshole, but whatever he had done, it wasn't bad enough to keep Lizzie away from him. Nigel was to take care of Lizzy while Ruby was in New York looking. I guess this was more of the leaving in her, and later, looking back, I guess she'd been leaving most of her life.

Well, Ruby needed a break, after all her selfless giving, she felt entitled, and damn she was. The girl worked her whole life without a break, and Nigel was Lizzie's father, and it was his turn to take care of her, so Ruby up and left, and landed on New York's waiting shores.

One thing about Ruby, one thing about her sadness was that she couldn't stick with just one decision. Me, I didn't like having regrets, so early on in my life, I figured that when I made a decision, I would go with it. You weigh the alternatives, you consider the consequences, you make your decision, and you dive in it, head first. I had known too many assholes who spent their lives in regret. Frank Smith, back in Connecticut used to always wish he had done something different. *"I shoulda asked her out!"*... *"I almost punched him out!"*... *"I was so close to..."*

Frank Smith woulda never done anything different, and deep down inside himself Frank Smith knew it.

***

Frank Smith would never admit it, and maybe to himself, maybe somewhere deep down inside he knew it. Me, I tend to think that everyone gets what they really want. Frank Smith always wanted to be that close to something without actually getting it. I had to believe that was exactly how he wanted it. Frank Smith had fear, and "almost" was about as close as he really wanted to get to taking chances.

I used to stir Ruby up by asking her why she chose to be so sad, and she'd get pissed off and said that she didn't understand how I could ask something so cruel. She insisted that no one deserved to be as unhappy as she was, and why in her right mind should she choose to be that way. Since Ruby didn't think it could be fixed, I had to assume that that was her way of making it so. It may not be my place to say it, but maybe Ruby didn't choose to be sad, maybe she just chose to stay that way.

So Ruby left Elizabeth with Nigel to follow a dream. Ruby however, always chose to remain sad and never forgave herself. She made that decision and like so many others she had made prior, found this was another one she just couldn't live with. It didn't take her long in New York to realize that she was not a party girl anymore, or maybe she never was, yet she thought that maybe this was one of the things that she had been missing out on all these years.

By the time Ruby came to me, she was starting to see that she had made another bad decision in her life. She missed Elizabeth, and I can't blame her one bit. Ruby had left Nigel and Ruby wanted us all to be together. I saw that it was her on that dark New York night who made me feel special gain, and I guess I did to her as well. Whatever it was she saw in me, I guess part of it was that I wasn't one of those undiscovered self-appreciated assholes that seemed to find their way into every bar on the Lower East Side, and in spite of all the bad shit down there, I had maintained my self-respect, and I still believed in right and wrong, in good over evil.

***

Me, I came to New York eight years earlier, 'cause there was no other place to go. Coming from Connecticut did have something to do with it, but I had always felt that my birthplace was of no major consequence. I was taught right from wrong, but I was also spoon-fed a whole lotta socially-correct horseshit that never made any sense to me, so good-riddance. None of us really have the choice to pick where it is we're gonna come into this world, and we are just born where we are born. The souls have to come out where the souls come out.

Ruby was a soul who was placed where she didn't belong. The Lord must've had a reason for placing her where she was. Maybe she was being punished for something she did in another life. There always seems to be a lotta "maybe" involved in thinking too much. The Ruby I knew, however, did not deserve one ounce of the shit that had been thrown her way. Ruby was a martyr. She never actually came out and said it, but her actions dictated otherwise. Ruby would give and give and give. Ruby suffered for the poor little children. Ruby would fight the good fight, but fight was all she knew. I asked her once why she fought so much. Ruby told me that her fight was all she had. I admired her for that and I pitied her for that. The trouble was, Ruby could find a fight where there wasn't one. There's always inequality, and Ruby saw no fairness, no justice, everywhere she looked. Sometimes things got to her so much that nothing else mattered. Sometimes, most of the time, Ruby would fight just to fight.

Ruby used to say that you couldn't choose your parents. We souls, we were born into families and situations we couldn't help. Me, I was always an outsider and perhaps that is why I never felt my place back in Connecticut. I never would've chose it if I had my way. I've always believed in right and wrong. I'd stick my neck out for what's right, I'd lay everything on the line. I'd do anything for that which is right and I'd do anything for Love.

***

Back in Connecticut, they used to tell me I was "too sensitive". It was hard to realize my own creativity when the sin of being too sensitive was the other side of that same creativity. Hell, I see sensitivity is the whole ball of wax, you see the beauty and you see the shit. The artist sees it all. She used to say how proud of me she was, she used to show my art to the friends and neighbors, she used to brag on how creative I was, *but son, you're too sensitive, slow down now and stop all that foolishness. Why can't you just be like everyone else?*

I guess I am too sensitive. It keeps me awake at night, it shakes me up in the daytime, it pisses me off and sends me off on a frenzy. Sometimes it rocks my soul, the way I thought that Ruby's should have been rocked. I think New York to me was a way of cutting down on the sensitivity. That goes without saying. Either you desensitize or you explode. I guess I could never fully let go of it. I guess I sorted it out, and saved it for those that really needed it. I stopped muggings, broke up fights, fed the homeless, but I knew where to draw the line. Ruby, she suffered for the children, she felt that pity. Ruby, she wanted to save everyone, the way no one had been there to save her. Ruby, poor gal, however, didn't know how to shut it off. Ruby lived it seemed, only to fight.

I swore after one too many heartbreaks, that I wasn't gonna feel anyone else's pain ever again. I guess we're all human though, and that's an easy position to take from a distance. All the misogynist machos who go on with their, *"bitches this"* and *"bitches that"*...are revealing how close they really got. That's the easy way out. Old and jaded as I am, I still try to keep them all separate, and see each one as new and different, and not to take out past misery on the next one who enters my life.

***

Sometimes I don't know if Ruby ever really saw who I was. I would have to assume that she saw it at first, but the cloud of her father and of all those others started getting in her eyes. Because she had once been mistaken for another, she thought that I too, was making the same mistake. I don't think it was possible to mistake her for another...Ruby was one of a kind, but she'd get all torn up and start ragging on *"men this,"* and *"men that,"* and it was men's fault why things were so fucked up, and Lord, did she carry around some anger. Me and Ruby, maybe we were too much alike. I wasn't gonna let her cheat herself this way without a fight. I was gonna challenge her, make her think, and maybe, just maybe save her from herself. Damn, was I naïve...

***

Ruby would get emotional and go on a tirade about all that men were. I ended up getting pushed into a corner, getting the brunt of all this, all the while keeping my cool. When things'd calm down, I'd say, *"Ruby you know you are a brilliant woman whom I respect and you know there's no one else like you, but you get on this high horse and you really cheat yourself. Ruby, you are otherwise brilliant until you start talking about men...and girl, if you replace the word "Black" or "Mexican" or even "Woman" every time you use that word "Men," you'd realize what a bigot you really are!"*

Well all that made sense to me, and the way I look back on it, it was the truth, or the truth the way I saw it. Maybe if she was anyone else she would've listened. Maybe if she was anyone else, she wouldn't have been so angry. Maybe we are all animals, we don't have a choice in the world, and maybe I was pissing in the wind, playing Leave It To Beaver one more time. Ruby wanted no part of it, Ruby had her mind made up and maybe it was the Irish on her Daddy's side, and maybe it was the Texas she was born into, but don't ever tell that girl she's wrong about anything.

***

Back in New York, Helen Fisk asked me why I was so much in love with Ruby. Now Helen never had much luck with men. As a matter of fact, Helen never had much luck with anything. Helen couldn't make a decision, and the decisions she did make were usually wrong. Helen seemed to be in a constant state of confusion. Helen had a husband she didn't much care for, couldn't get rid of, but probably never made that point too clear to him. Helen kept riding that safe place right in the middle, right on top of the fence, probably because everything she thought she wanted to change had become all too familiar to her. Somehow I see that situation way back then as being all too similar to what ended up happening between me and Ruby.

As quick as Helen asked me why I was so much in love with Ruby, it came right out, clear as the night sky. Without another thought, I replied, *"I like waking up with her!"* Well Helen didn't think that was much of a reason for two people to be together, and Helen was too cynical to want to understand what I was saying to her. She probably thought about how uncomfortable she was with physical closeness, the unpleasantness of morning breath and waking up with hair so wild, no man should see. She probably thought about the last man she woke up with and how she had all these regrets about the night before and swore it would never happen again. Well, me, I'm a romantic. I loved waking up with Ruby, I liked her closeness next to mine. I loved feeling her heart beat, that heartbeat that kept that sweet angel ticking. Waking up with Ruby reminded me of falling in her arms the night before, the last face I'd see before the infinity of sleep, the first one I'd see in the early morning Sun. Waking up with Ruby reminded me of starting every new day fresh with her, of going into the future together, and of not looking back. Waking up with Ruby made me think of nothing else but going forward, ever forward.

***

I used to run a small construction crew back there, putting up fences. New York is a funny place that way, you're either putting up fences to keep people in, or putting up fences to keep people out. From Rikers Island to Bushwick, Brooklyn, this continued to prove true. We kept putting up fences and people on either side of those fences tended to be pretty scary.

Usually on our way out of town, we'd sit in the truck on the Williamsburg Bridge, sitting dead still in rush hour traffic. Most of the bridges were built back when there was money in the tills and politicians knew it was wise to cough a little back to the people. Well those days had passed, and those bridges were falling, usually little bits at a time. The Williamsburg Bridge, hell, they'd shut down two roadways in either direction, just to take a little stress off, but we all knew it was gonna fall someday.

Me, I'd sit on that bridge, dead still, waiting in traffic, and sometimes that bridge would sway and sometimes it would buckle, and I just sat there wondering if I'd be on it on that one day when it did cave in. It didn't matter much to me, I had no death wish, but neither did I fear death. I just wondered if I'd be on it when it fell.

After I met Ruby, one big thing I felt, was suddenly I feared death. I don't know so much if I feared it, as much as I didn't look forward to it the same way. All of a sudden I had a reason to live, someone to come home to, someone to provide for. It may have been growing up, or it may have been settling down, but damn, if that girl didn't make me wanna live, live to wake up with her again, and again, and face the future together. Helen Fisk had no idea.

Me and Ruby ran around New York like a couple of kids. I let her spoil me when I probably shouldn't have. I was low on bucks in those days and she had a pretty good job. I shoulda said no, but I let her take me all around, feed me, get me drunk, and then we'd come home and climb up on each other's hospitality. Then I'd wake up with her again.

***

New York was grinding on both of us back then. Me, I had been there eight years and Ruby should have never came, except to find me. She used to marvel at how our paths had crossed so many times before we ever met. Ruby's brother lived in the building next to mine and in a small town New York neighborhood, where everyone ended up at the same place, sometimes at the same time, I'd never met the man. Her brother's girlfriend was in the apartment on the other side of the wall from mine. Right there, so near. All the times Ruby came to visit and was there, just a heartbeat away and neither one of us knew. Perhaps that was symbolic of the tragedy me and Ruby were to face in this world, being so near and being so far. And Ruby, back then, Ruby believed in Karma.

Well time was passing and the time came when we decided to move away. Ruby grew up in a military family, moving around year after year. Born in Texas, was the only place Ruby called home. Me, I always liked Texas...had been there a few times. I had no real roots in Connecticut, and New York was home for a while. Texas was there, just short of Mexico. Things were going to shit, and if the bottom dropped out, I wanted to be that close to Mexico, just in case. It was time to move on.

Me and Ruby started making plans to get Lizzy, and move on down to Texas. It's possible that none of what was about to happen would have happened if we had stayed in New York, but Texas called us. I guess being animals with no real control over our actions, with the stars being our motivation, we went west, and there was nothing that would have dictated otherwise.

***

I dreamt about Ruby last night. I wish I could say it was good dream, I can't really say it was bad, just kinda disturbing I suppose.

I spoke to Ruby recently on the telephone. We were civilized, hell, we were touching something in one another, even if it was just commiserating over the way things had been and the way things had become. Well it showed me that there was hope, hope of seeing some things eye-to-eye, hope of maybe getting back together. Now I really wanna believe that, especially after the way Ruby was dumping all of her shit on me, trying to make me the bad guy in the ongoing drama of her life. She tried so hard to pretend she was scared of me, physically scared, and scared I was out to rip her off. She told me that she took responsibility for leaving, but in reality, she was too far over her head in guilt, and had to come clean by making someone else the villain. I needed her back for vindication, if nothing else.

Something about Ruby I thought was sad and unnecessary was how she always had to take the blame for everything. I never much cared for the saying "shit happens", but sometimes it does. Sometimes shit just does happen. Poor Ruby had to have someone to blame for all the shit that happened. She had to blame someone else, or else it was her who was to blame, it didn't really matter who it was, there had to be a bad guy. I only started to realize it back then. At the time, it seemed that me and Ruby both believed in right and wrong. The trouble was that I believed that the concept of right and wrong meant there was a "Good Guy", the one who would make things right. Ruby took it to mean there was a "Bad Guy", the one who was to blame for all the world's wrongs. Ruby just had too many bad guys in her life. Ruby's life was full of villains, I don't blame her, it wasn't her fault. In a perfect world, Ruby would've let go of 'em a long time ago, but from an early age, Ruby learned there were villains. Ruby learned there were demons. I think she may have softened over time, though. From an early age she carried the horror with her and the knowledge that there was no way out, that it couldn't be fixed and she seemed to do a good job living with it all. If it wasn't villains, it was demons, who came in unannounced, uninvited and they crept into that little girl's room late that night, and they forced themselves upon her, they forced themselves inside of her, they were pushed deep into her soul, and that poor angel was never to trust again, not in herself, not in anyone else, and certainly not in any man.

***

Me, I was different. Me, I saw those demons, I knew those demons. I did just about everything but talk to those demons…that was up to her. I think the one thing that would have fixed things was if Ruby could have talked to her demons. She knew 'em, and she knew 'em well. She knew when they came in, and how long they had been there, uninvited, but that's where it ended. She couldn't face 'em, couldn't look 'em in the eye, and could never talk to 'em. Ruby had fear. Those demons scared her so much to death, all she could do was let 'em lay there, inside her and by her side. She let her demons revel in the sheer torture they inflicted on her, and she reveled in the fact that that was all she let 'em have, that she could still move on.

Ruby was tough. Sometimes her toughness was a mask, but usually it was real. Those demons made her tough. The trouble was they scared the life out of her, too. Without those demons, she woulda been tough, but in a different kinda way. I loved her toughness. I worshipped her toughness, but I resented that she had to be tough against me as well. Hell, I was no threat, I did what I had to do, but I never did anything against her. Anything I did that made her scared was only what I did to protect her, but those demons told her otherwise. I just wish she coulda been as tough against those demons. The trouble is with people, any people really, is that those that got the least cause to feel bad about themselves, are usually the ones that do it to themselves. Sometimes I felt Ruby was tough because of her deep fear that she was not that tough. If that girl could've seen herself the way that I had seen her, seen her in all her glory, she wouldn't have had fear at all.

Ruby made me think that it's just like jumping into a cold lake early in the morning. She just had to take a deep breath, close her eyes, release the fear, and jump right on into the cold, clear water. She wasn't gonna drown, she wasn't gonna stop breathing...shit I knew she could've jumped into that cold lake, and I realized how much she really could rise to the surface and swim. In my mind, Ruby was so tough, she could've looked right in the eye of those demons, talked right at them, told those demons to get the hell out, and I may be simplifying things, but if she had that awareness within herself, she could've been a happy woman. If Ruby could've seen Ruby the way I seen Ruby, if Ruby could've seen her demons the way I did. *If only, if only...*

***

So in my dream, I was driving the Rent-a-Truck just like I did from Albuquerque to bring her and Lizzie those things, and to say good-bye. Damn, was I noble. I wouldn't have had it any other way. From the day I finally got her on the phone, I was devastated. I took all the hollow points out of that .45, 'cause it scared me how good that barrel felt up around my face and forehead. I know a permanent and irreversible decision when I'm holding it in my hand, so I figured maybe things would work out better if I put the bullets in the other room.

So I'm dreaming I'm in that Rent-a-Truck all alone and sad, driving on down that road to who-knows-where, and then I'm out on a mesa walking down a bank of stone steps, descending like I did that day out there in the Ancient City, the day I had that feeling, the day I wished they were there with me, but somehow knew deep down inside that they had left. Sometime after climbing down the rocks, there she was in that room, and me wanting an answer, but she had no answer for me. She was scared, but still played it tough. She told me that she and he had fucked six times the night before, and she was feeling like a kid again, without a care in the world, and she didn't really have to know anymore what was going on. Ruby was free now and I was alone.

I guess I asked for it. I was looking for problem resolution and that was what I was given. I still do believe in truth, though. Over all the years, and all the disappointments I do know one thing about truth. Truth may not be apparent at any one point in time, but truth does come out over the passage of time.

***

Ruby was letting things go. She only needed to be responsible for herself and Lizzie now. She was being the child she was never allowed to be. The basic male ego may have said, *"fuck it, she's gone"*, but I never hung around in locker rooms. Male ego is a contradictory thing and the tough male image usually was the result of some high school sweetheart who broke his heart maybe a decade ago. Me, I got over it.

It was different in Texas. In Texas, people got married, unmarried, separated, divorced, remarried, re-divorced, an' them that been together the longest couldn't usually remember if they were still married or not. In Texas, nothing was over 'til it was over.

I will not love someone to my own self-destruction, but I will love for the salvation of all. Letting Ruby go was the best thing I could've done for her, but hell, I want her back. I want her back so bad my guts hurt. I don't sleep, and if I don't write it down, I forget to eat. For some strange reason, I still possess a happiness for her searching. I want her to find, and to savor everything she'd been denied. If I never was to see her again, I could rest quiet, hoping that she found that happiness that had eluded her for so long.

Well my dream told me that she was out there, that she was still looking and that the answer was not here, but somewhere further down the road. I guess I still got enough of that Connecticut problem resolution in me to believe in answers, and every time I close my eyes and pray, every time I focus every bit of my energy on her, and every time I meditate on her happiness, I feel that some of that energy is going her way. For now, Ruby's got to be alone.

***

Back on Ludlow Street, I was "Whiteboy" and had been since Dad died and I quit my job. The tag came from playing in a band back in the early 80s. All the white assholes were trying so hard to be black. *"Black people are so cool...Black people gots rhythm, white people are so uptight!"* Well I got no particular affinity toward any one group. I distrust blacks in large groups same as I distrust whites in large groups. The souls are just born into it. It has nothing to do with birthright, heritage, lineage, race or social class. We are just born into it. White people, though, well white people are what Connecticut is all about. Those Puritans got off the boat in God's chosen land and the stubborn bastards just never left.

Whiteboy was an identity. It was a way of saying who I was, making fun of race, making fun of suburban whiteness, making fun of blacks, darks and browns and everyone in-between. It was about being honest, and havin' a sense of humor. Life is too short, most of everything that hangs people up is based on imaginary lines anyway. Chill out and enjoy the ride. Well, that's too simple for most people. Most people wanna be separate, wanna be miserable, wanna be too intellectual, wanna read too much into something, and wanna read too much.

Whiteboy had balls, Krylon-breathing, out alone in scary land at three in the morning balls. There was nothing like fat-cap tagging on some fresh walls out in the middle of nowhere when out of the dark you hear…

"Yo! What's you write?"

Turn around, make contact, stand firm, smile, and reply,

"Whiteboy!"

Nothing aggressive, just a question followed by an answer. Brothers' a little nervous all of a sudden.

"Shit man, this motherfucker's crazy, leave 'im alone, let's jus' get the fuck outa here!"

Sometimes "Whiteboy" was a ticket out of a whole lot of trouble.

There was nothing racist about it. Fuck racism. White liberals hated it. White liberals want to be pissed off. Sensitive and caring white guilty liberals wanted to have someone to blame. They wanted to be part of the solution, in their mind. I've got no problem with anyone, and I would stand up for anyone, but you gotta have a sense of humor. You gotta smile. It was funny, white guilty liberals would get up in my face and give me all kinda shit about some kind of white supremacist bullshit or some other abstract evil they were trying to point their finger at. "Whiteboy" offended them and "Whiteboy" scared them. They weren't that deep and it didn't take long to set them honkies straight...

"Bitch, they don't call you Whiteboy back in Connecticut, they don't call you Whiteboy at the country club or on the tennis courts. Shit, listen...they call you Whiteboy back in Brooklyn, up in Harlem, down here on the Lower East Side." They don't usually have the ghetto balls to call it to your face, it's usually once you've walked past 'em, but they say it down here, nonetheless."

One white guilty woman got up in my face about me offending the entire black race, and something about being a brick in the "complicity" that was *"keeping them down"* and so forth. She went on and on and on 'til she started pissing me off just a little.

"You know the blacks have no problem with it. The Puerto Ricans and Dominicans have no problem with it, but you do. If I wrote "Zippy One" on the walls, you wouldn't have spent any of this time talking to me, but "Whiteboy" got you thinking for maybe the last ten minutes and I don't know...when was the last time you thought about anything?"

White guilty woman got all pissed off and stormed off, but I made her think.

***

There is a subtle art in being able to shut those narrow-minded white guilty liberals up, even for a couple of seconds. Over-education and self-importance is a dangerous thing. I did my part by making one of 'em think, however briefly. Everyone should be made to think for a few minutes at least once in their life. Make 'em think…

***

So Dad died back in August of '88. Grandma died in August of '88, and Uncle Rich died shortly after. Cindy didn't want to see me again, and back then I thought I'd be with her forever. Cindy, one day, just stopped sleeping with me, stopped talking to me, wouldn't acknowledge my existence, and after two years of what I thought was close intimacy, would not even tell me why. The rug had been pulled out from under me in a bad way, and I spent about three weeks laying on the floor on Valium, teevee, and cigarettes, studying every line and crack on that ninety-year old tenement ceiling. It was an extended, self-induced hypnotic stupor that kept me from doing any serious harm. Back in those days, I was making my money selling art and T-shirts, and at some point of awareness, I came to realize that if I didn't get up off the floor someday soon, I might just be doing the same thing on the street. The anger and energy built up and built up until it got me back on my feet, painting the walls at night, and Whiteboy roamed those dark and dirty streets, shit-faced and half crazy, most nights 'til dawn. From my brain and my heart, out through my hands to those paint-soaked walls, I let the anger and agony out for all to see.

***

It started out, I was in such pain back then, I'd get free-drinks drunk most of the night, back then when I knew most of the bartenders, and scary, I could drink most of the time, all night long for free. It didn't take long though, to realize that no drink was gonna take away the pain. So I'd go back to my place, climb the four flights of ninety-year-old stairs and fill up that big old plastic milk crate with buckets, rollers, brushes, cans and whatever else, and head over to junkie land. Second Street was my favorite spot at that time, by two or three in the morning, the store had closed, and most of the junkies were passed out and pissed on. Cops didn't really wanna be there anyway, so sure as shit, once the store was closed and everyone had moved on, they really didn't wanna lay eyes on any of it, let alone walk through it.

It was like making love, it was like fucking that wall. That old building, all tore up, bricked over, just waiting for the wrecking ball, torched years ago by landlord too overwhelmed to care and ready to cash in. Wall was covered with lots of tags, but that's why I brought the bucket of white…roll over that shit, oil-based, wet on wet, get out those four inch brushes, no plan, no sketch, no idea 'til it came out, and burn out these scary primitive faces with red dripping eyes, from deep inside the subconscious. Emotional, pure and from the heart, in just a few minutes, a twelve by twelve foot wall, still pouring down on me, and I throw my shit back in that milk crate and roll off, covered in pure loving oil base. Not a thing the Man could or would do, and I was pure.

Folks down there liked it too. Regardless of their artistic inclination, it was better than looking at "Fuck You" and "Julio 69". Puerto Ricans and Dominicans, sitting outside in lawn chairs on dirty sidewalk, ice chest filled with cans of Bud, Salsa blaring on some cheap boom box resting on a sagging plastic milk crate. I used to tag "Muchacho Blanco" down there, out of respect for them, and they loved that. Crumbling bricks, junkies on the street or not, it was their home, and although I was uninvited, they let me come in to paint their outdoor living room. "Painting Without Permission"... "PWOP"...they loved it anyway. This was about as far away from Connecticut as a Whiteboy could get and things were good.

**

Back in those days, I had come to New York during a renaissance of sorts. At least downtown, everything, every square inch that could be covered with paint, was covered with paint. Everything from original, Old School Graffiti, bubble letters and blockbuster throw-ups, to Third-World murals to gang tags, full colored top-to-bottom murals and wanna-be art fag shit, and sometimes just walls splashed with paint, empty buckets littered the sidewalks. Lower East Side, "East Village", Alphabet City, the whole ball of wax, was a colorful Garden of Eden where anything could grow out of seemingly nothing.

I guess everything comes and goes in waves. Back then, lots of galleries Downtown, East Side, lots of slumming honkies high on coke with fear of their own white penis, thought it was cool to hang out Downtown with the homeboys. There was a lotta attitude you had to shovel to avoid stepping in it, but the overall effect was still mind fucking! The paint...the paint was amazing! There were posters too, wheat-pasted band posters, political posters, nihilistic, anarchistic, "Squat or Rot" posters, art prints, whatever. It was no one thing. It was the effect, the overall effect, the unconsciously collective effort, the layering of all of the different styles overlapping, layering one style to the other. Everyone conformed to succeed, but the great unconscious made sure that there was no conformity in the overall effect. Back in those days, anything went, and that's where Whiteboy got his earliest influence, where Whiteboy got his style. Anything goes...Fear nothing and move boldly forward.

***

I had a dream about Ruby last night. It wasn't really a dream. Since I met Ruby, I've had what I call visions. Somewhere, late at night, in between sleep and awake, I think with eyes closed, but still conscious of everything around me, and then Bam! Eyes open, heart pounding and a strange awareness, very vivid imagery and no mistaking the message. Sometimes it was situations, sometimes animals, once a voice so loud and clear, like it was standing right over me. I never had these before I met Ruby, and wondered if I ever would again. Maybe she's still with me in that way. Ruby was way spiritual, and damn, could she see things. Usually, though, her controlling side put too much doubt in her for her to really believe in her own visions.

So somehow or another, Ruby was in my arms, sobbing, just out of control in tears. We were holding each other like that's all there was left on Earth. We're pouring sweat so bad it's like every pore in our being was crying. Her eyes glistened as she sobbed, *"you've been so good to me, I don't know what went wrong, I don't know what I've done, I don't know why!"* I held her like I'd never let go, and she held me. I told her it was okay to come back, that I never let her go anyway, that I never stopped loving her.

I couldn't tell if she was really coming back. In my vision she wanted to. In my vision, it was the right thing. In a perfect world without sorrow and ego and stubbornness, in a world without damage and past lives, it was the right thing. My vision told me not what would happen, but what should happen for both of us. Most of all, my vision told me I had done the right thing.

Cliché or no, if you love her, you let her go. Damn it hurts, it hurts so much, but it's the right thing to do. One day I will hold her in my arms, and help her with her tears, but for now I let her go. I let her go, and it hurts so much...

***

Ruby wanted a dog. Before we even got to Texas, Ruby wanted some of the things only country living could afford. We were gonna have dogs, we were gonna have guns, we were gonna have a driveway so long that no one comes up to the house by accident. And Ruby had a dream about this dog. Long before we ever got to Texas, Ruby saw this dog and she knew it was hers.

After we got settled down in Rigler, the Animal Shelter was having a "Pet Fair." Come down and pick out your dog. Regan Frank was a real gentleman; retired airline pilot who lived on a ranch out in the county. He was a modern-day saint who took in all those strays, fed 'em and once in a while piled the whole pack all in a big old stock trailer, and brought 'em on into town to find everyone a good home. We went down that day, me and Ruby and Lizzie to find Ruby that dog. We were looking and petting and having a great old time, looking at all the dogs, all those dogs showing off, on their best behavior, looking for someone to take 'em home. Ruby looked around and pointed to one sitting in the back all alone and said, *"that one!"*

Bonnie, as we named her, was sitting there all alone, kind of scared and standoffish, kind of lonely, but dignified in her aloneness.

This was the dog that Ruby dreamt about. When I started to observe, I saw a lot of Ruby in that dog. She had been kicked and abused, but inside you could see her goodness. You could see what once was a trusting, caring soul. And just like Ruby, we brought that dog around and she started to trust again, and she started to let loose. She started to see that there was no danger. Bonnie was a metaphor for poor Ruby. I started to see them both come around. No one was kicking no one anymore, and there was no reason to cry, no reason to cower. We were starting to settle in and relax a bit. It looked like things were getting better.

***

Guns, I dunno, I never used to care for them, philosophically at least. I always liked the looks of them, the feel of them, always wanted to collect them. I just didn't really like the notion that you needed a gun to settle differences. Hell, I came to New York with a pocketful of switchblades, brass knuckles, chains, and just about any hand weapon that didn't load up with bullets. A warrior came back from another age. Crazy motherfuckers down in Chinatown used to love to sell these insane "Martial Arts" weapons. My Martial Arts brother thought he had all of them until this little bent-over, white-bearded Chinese man smiled, reached below the display case and pulled out a three section blowgun with a variety of darts, at no extra charge. Poison not included.

Me, I carried only in case I was ever cornered, ever outnumbered. Hell, I've been in fistfights, sometimes taking some hard licks, my hand within inches of whatever weapon I was carrying, but never pulled anything out. It was not necessary unless I was down and really needed it, that's the only time it would have really mattered. Ego was a whole other thing, and tough, insecure machos may like to flash weapons, but I never saw the need. Those hidden hand weapons probably dressed me in the air of self-confidence and fearlessness, and back there in New York, back there in those scary times, I wouldn't have gone out without 'em.

If I was still back there in New York, I would carry a gun at all times. Things have changed. It was early-mid eighties when I first landed there, and people used to tell me, *"Don't walk down such-and such street"*... *"Never go down Bedford Avenue at night"*... *"Here's the blocks you gotta avoid..."*... *"Man, they don' like white people down there!"* Blah Blah Blah...I had a shrink once tell me I was "counter-phobic". When I was told to fear something, when I was told to avoid something, sure as shit, I would end up there, I would walk right on into it and face it head-on. I guess that's one reason I left the safety and sameness of Connecticut.

People down there used to also say, *"be careful...you don't know if he's got a gun or not..."* Well, I couldn't see running around like every other asshole in the world was carrying a gun...what kind of life would that be? Well, I guess it may have been good advice, 'cause these days, every asshole in the world does have a gun, and I don't really appreciate what it's done to the balance of power. If I had to choose between hunter and hunted though, I'd have to choose hunter, with no second thought. I don't feel overly aggressive with a gun, I don't feel it will necessarily correct any wrong. I pretty much just carry with the secure knowledge that I am not the hunted in this world. I did go to say good-bye to Ruby with a loaded pistol. Just in case.

***

The first gun I bought was that big Colt .45 revolver. We were living way out in the country and I was working nights. Those dogs had a mean bark, and Charlie, the second one, the puppy, would just light on into something without a second thought. Hell, him and Bonnie would stand their ground in the middle of the night, even when the coyotes would come around. Dogs are faithful that way.

There was still something about a warm gun, especially a warm gun in Ruby's hands alone at night when I was away. The thing about guns is that there is no humane way to use 'em. A sonofabitch comes into your house, or comes at you, and you wanna stop him right where he is, a .22 is fine for targets, but me, the bigger the better, and that ol' .45 with those big, no-fooling around hollow points would rip a hole in a metal sign, about an inch wide. Motherfucker comes in the house at night, I think that would be the best way to keep everyone safe and maintain the balance of power.

Ruby used to love that gun. I came home one night about three in the morning, and there she was, out in the driveway, wearing just shorts and her boots, her gorgeous white torso shining under the Moon's dull glow. She was holding that gun with both hands, feet planted firmly on the ground, and firing away into the darkness. Ruby said a pack of wild dogs had been circling the house, and she was worried that they were there to take Charlie away with 'em. Well I looked at Ruby, pistol in her hand, beautiful white breasts heaving in the moonlight as she took deep breaths, eyes piercing into the darkness, and I guess a girl's gotta have a hobby, and I suppose this one was as good as any. I went inside for a beer.

One other night, I came in from work, about four in the morning. I took my time in the kitchen, had one or two beers, grabbed a bite, and was shuffling around some, I guess. Well I hadn't noticed, but it seems that Ruby had called out, which I didn't hear, so that whole time I was out there in the kitchen, she was sitting up in the bed, back to the wall, pointing that sonofabitch .45 right at the door. Well me, I walked in and saw my loving wife pointing that big ol' gun right at my chest, hoping there was no hidden motivation. I smiled, and said *"it's okay Babe, it's me!"*

Jim Watson from Houston was married to a crazy woman too, maybe most of us were back then. He walked into the same situation one night, late at night coming home drunk from the bar, and when he walked in and saw her face over that threatening gun barrel, and said, *"it's not Jim!"* Whatever was really going on in her head, the only thing I can say for sure is that Ruby was indeed pointing that big ol' gun at me.

***

Back to Whiteboy. Whiteboy may or may not have been a big deal. Trouble with all that shit, is that it started out pure and simple. It started out with raw emotion tearing up the walls, blowing off all that steam. Then, sure enough, you get that old New York bullshit in the back of your mind. Rich and famous had never been high on my list, but there's still something about it that will nag away at you from a distance. In New York, as a rule, at least as an artist, you didn't make it, you didn't get rich, until you were famous.

Me, I've seen artists do it...get a name for themselves, then people would seek them out, seek out their services, seek out their uniqueness, then they could write their own ticket, go right on their way... This was all subliminal, in those days it was a gradual transition. Artists claim purity, but artists are the ultimate Capitalists. *"I just can't afford his work anymore"* is a sure sign that one is on their way. I didn't see it at first, but what plans are made that are ever kept? I guess the purity doesn't last long in any scenario. I only had enough emotion to do so many walls...to fuck those walls with that soulful purity that don't come around that often and don't last all that long either.

***

The propensity to conform raises its ugly head, when you least expect it. There have been times I have detested non-conformists for their intense efforts to remain perpetually different. At some point, their non-conformity has lost its purity and seems to be no more than an extension of the ego, an inability to roll with the changing times. Maybe it's the only way to stay off the main path, I'm still not sure. Me, I've been different my whole life. Every now and then, I've found myself straying towards the comforting veil of conformity. Beside those big primitive faces, dripping wet, I'd roll around downtown with a sack fulla spray paint, mostly tagging, but usually leaving some message to rise above the rest, to avoid the conformity that was becoming all too common in street Graffiti.

"WHITEBOY NO RHYTHM"... "WHITEBOY NO TOMORROW"... "PREPARE YOUR BURIAL SHROUD"... the Demise was always right around the corner.

"NO ONE REIGNS"... "CHILL THE FUCK OUT"... "OWTA FUCKIN' CONTROL"... life was always outa control so you may as well enjoy the ride.

"SUBLIMINAL MINDFUCK"...in Krylon gold, you could only see it on those metal pull-down gates if the streetlight was hitting it just right...just to warn them assholes to watch out, and then it was gone.

"PAINTING WITHOUT PERMISSION"... "KONKRETE AMERICA WITH A DOORMAN"... on the front of that new high-rent coop down in SoHo with Yuppie assholes trying to be near the soul of the city, all the while evicting the soulful because they couldn't keep up with the new lifestyle, or the new cost of living, and definitely couldn't afford the wardrobe. That morning about seven o'clock, I came back to photograph the damage, perhaps to photocopy and start an ongoing mailing to the residents of that out-of-place SoHo palace where warehouses and factories once stood, where people actually used to work with their hands and there I was, covered in paint, the same colors as were on the wall, still reelin' from the fumes in place of air to breathe, and as I roll around the corner with my camera ready, there is the building Super, talking to the cops, who are taking extensive notes, and photographs to identify the style, and an army of pissed-off looking painters with rollers, and drop cloths all over the sidewalk, and I decided it would be best to savor that mental picture, to savor the impermanence of the act, and get the fuck off the block fast.

***

They say it's all about the names, but it was always more than that. *"Look at me!"* has always been the predominant statement of the human condition. Graffiti proliferated in the inner cities because of the impersonal nature of the modern world; it screamed out of alienation, it was a crime that kept the taggers from committing real crime. It was dogs pissing, and we're all animals anyway, so I can only say that the indignation comes from those who deny our animal connection.

The first thing you had to do was to stand out, to justify the criminal act. You were not a social vandal if you were afraid. Graffiti was only a crime in the mind of the good upstanding citizen. In the future, when they dig up whatever's left of this place where we once lived, they are gonna see all the gold, and brass, and marble up in midtown, and say, *"some egotist built a monument to himself again!"* When they dig through the rubble that used to be the Lower East Side, that used to be Harlem, that used to be the South Bronx or Bed-Stuy, they're gonna see this indecipherable scribble, and they're gonna spend years, maybe lifetimes, trying to figure out what the common man, the alien, what the artist had to say.

You had to stand out, you had to stand your ground. It was underground, and it was anonymous, but there were all these scared little shits running around, talking big, acting like they ran everything, but they'd spray a little paint, looking all the while over their shoulders, and run away scared, later coming back, bragging to their homeboys how they fucked that wall up. Shit, you just had to take a deep breath, and go for it. One time I bombed a wall, mid-afternoon, as soon as the cop, walking his beat was just a few steps away from it. "CRACK BREAK HEAD" in block letters, ten-by-eight feet, Ultra-Flat Black on white I rolled-out the night before. Me, I would look around, just once, take a deep breath, then let the spirit flow. I'd take another breath, and there I was, kind of like Ruby jumping in that cold lake. You just gotta decide to do it, and go. If you're gonna break the law, then do it! Defy authority, and make a big splash while you do it. Don't put fear into your work, don't fuck the system wearing a rubber. Never show fear. Take a deep breath and jump in that lake. *Jump in that lake, Ruby.*

***

I expect a call from Ruby any day now. I hate to say it, I hate to even think it. It goes against everything I believe in, philosophically. Philosophically, shit...what is that anyway? From a distance back in the day, I used to say I was *"ready for anything, but expected nothing."* So now I'm here, expecting a call from Ruby. Shit, I already got the call, I'm still getting the call. Hell, I know, she doesn't even know she told me, but she told me...she doesn't know why she left, she doesn't know what she's doing back there in Rigler. Last time she called, she was confused, but this was something she had to do. Something she had to do. We're all on some course, and the illusion of making personal decisions can't do anything to alter that. Having control is fleeting, so it's best to revel in the brief glimmer of security while it lasts.

Last time I heard from Ruby, she was mad and yelled at me, of course not for the first time. *"You don't think it's gonna work between me and Skeeter, do you?"* I hate to dig too deep, but if I was outa the picture, out of her life forever, why the fuck did she care what the hell I thought about anything? As a matter of fact, I never said anything like that to her, though I knew it as plain as the hand in front of my face. I had no reason to really express any feelings to her after she left me, and I guess her screaming confession said it all. So she's already made that call, she already told me what's really going on. Trouble is, I come from Connecticut. Me, I want simple problem resolution. I wanna hear, *"I made a mistake, I'm sorry, I wanna come back to you!"* I already know she's made that call in her mind. Me, I've already picked up the message. I just don't wanna reach too far, for all the times Ruby up and left on me, this time she's gotta make the call, this time she's gotta come back to me.

***

It hurts, it hurts so bad, and it seems like there should be an easier way, but it was her decision to leave and it will be her decision to come back. I can't say I'm being noble, I'm probably just being realistic, but that's the only stake I've got in it at this point. Some have said to me that I gotta show her I love her, I gotta show her I care, to go back to Texas and to take her back. I probably could…for a while. I think the strongest thing I could have done is what I already had done, to let her know I'm there, to step back and do nothing else. If we belong together, she'll be back, and if I'm to have anything to do with her ever again, then she's gonna have to be the one to come back.

So me, I'm noble, or realistic, or whatever and I'm hurt…I'm hurt real bad. Every day I'm without Ruby I'm hurt. When we were still together, but she was away for a while, she was still by my side. I'd wake up in the morning with her in my arms, in the arms in my heart. I still feel her heartbeat, I still feel her in my heart, but am starting to wonder if I am no longer in hers.

I guess that waking up and facing the new day with her made everything all right. Now she's waking up with another, and nothing is all right. I miss Ruby, and she really ain't gonna see it until her thing starts to slow down, when the passion of the new and the strange wears out, but pretty soon, she's gonna be lonely too.

***

I've never done anything worthwhile that wasn't painful. Life is not a pleasant experience. Life can be full of wonderful, exciting experiences. You can transcend and feel the glory of the Universe, but you always come back down to where you were placed. There is always an equal and opposite reaction. I don't think they feel pain back there in Connecticut. God placed those Puritans there in New England and God keeps 'em from hurting, from feeling any pain, from facing any of the harsh reality. They don't usually stray too far from home, they pick obedient women that worship them and obey them. *"Honey, I don't want you to wear that sweater to the party tonight, and could you please do something else with your hair!"* While that sentiment would be construed as aggressive anywhere else, it's not anything out of the ordinary back there in New England where everything is perfect. Everything is as God planned.

Now I'm not saying that there's no pain back east, but there seems to be a natural tranquilizer flowing through them, that keeps 'em calm and even, because they choose not to pay attention, not to pay closer attention, not to get too close to anything that may cause a reaction. There are times when the pain actually does come through, but they are in no way prepared to deal with it. Reality is foreign and frightening, but for some reason, they are too composed and reserved to one day shoot up that Walmart. To me..to me, life is painful. Life is beautiful and life is painful. It is two sides of that same coin. Without beauty, there is no pain. Everything is equal and everything is opposite.

So being with Ruby wasn't painful, no more than anything else that was worth pursuing. It was dramatic; Ruby had a flair for the dramatic. From her history, the embodiment of affection always culminated in some type of drama or another. Hell, it was always exciting, but that pain, that pain that is out there in life…and to avoid it, or the threat of it, is to deny yourself that primary experience that may be the one thing that does in fact, separate us from the animals, or perhaps makes us just like them.

***

Well Ruby, she threw me away plain and simple, I suppose like an empty cigarette pack. It wasn't trash until she smoked all she cared to smoke. I'm entitled to the self-pity…the damn girl ran off, she let me go over the phone, once I finally found her, and she had no other excuses to make. She played it like she was scared of me, but with no real cause. Of course it was my fault. Everything was always someone else's fault in Ruby's world. It was always the fault of others, nothing was ever her fault. Ruby couldn't see her demons like I could, so she could only survive by blaming those around her. Me, I was in it for the long haul. Ruby, she thought she was in it for the long haul, too, trouble is she didn't stop to think about how long forever really was.

Everything on this Earth is fucked up and it's fucked up due to the existence of men, at least that's what Ruby said. What her Daddy had done to her, how he had done her Mother, what Nigel was supposed to have done to her, and all those poor gals, husbands up and leaving 'em for hot younger things, younger things all the time. *"Men only leave when they have another one, a better one, a younger one on the line,"* Ruby used to say. Well, by the time I finally found Ruby on the phone and she told me it was over, she had already lined up the next man in her life. Fierce and independent to herself, in her own eyes, fierce and independent, she thought to the world, but I was startin' to see Ruby…in truth, was still Daddy's little girl.

Maybe in my Connecticut naiveté, I believed Ruby, maybe in a perfect world that's what you do, you believe the one you love. The truth is that if I thought about it too much, or if I thought about what her anger was really about, I started to see how much her father had made her who she was, how much she had grown up in his image, and what he had turned her into. Her constant anger, her hatred of men, her hatred of her father, why couldn't she let any of it go? It became so obvious all of a sudden how much her father was a part of her...she knew it, and she couldn't let it go. Poor Ruby...She hated her father and she hated herself.

***

I never looked for the pain. Pain is a relative thing. Your basic he-man will inflict pain on himself in the weight room, in the tattoo parlor, in a fist fight, on the field of battle, but can that he-man take the real pain, the pain that life dishes out, the pain for which there is no script, no instruction, no warning? Back when I was a head-banger, not one of these long-haired heavy metal pussies, who flails his hair to the over-volumed wailings of some lead guitarist's ego, but a real hard-core punk rock head-banger...I think I liked the pain. Getting bashed in the pit, during GBH, The DKs or the Bad Brains, you gotta stay on your feet. You gotta stay on your feet to keep the muggers away. Back to the wall, and nowhere to go, you drive your razor sharp spiked bracelet into your forehead and smile, a little blood trickling down your face. *"Shit man, this motherfucker's crazy, we ain't gonna get paid here, let's get the fuck outa here!"*

I thought I was a bad ass, but I had a roommate back in Brooklyn. KG was an intellectual, a minor musical genius. He was shy and reserved, but an astute observer of the human condition. After seeing me coming back from countless CBGBs matinees, face-offs with muggers, and my seemingly overall disregard for personal safety, KG approached me one day and said, *"you like pain, but it's controlled pain that you like!"* I hadn't really confronted it myself, but shit…that Indiana frat boy was right, Pain wasn't so bad if you could anticipate it, prepare for it, and bask in its brilliance, but it's the pain you aren't prepared for that hurts so much.

I never really felt pain when I was with Ruby, she was the one who had the pain. I understood her sadness, I saw her pain, and of course I felt some of it, but it would have been physically impossible to feel all of that girl's pain without completely falling apart, so I endured.

***

Thoughts of killing invade my sanity lately. Once those thoughts come around though, nothing seems insane about it. Killing is a perfectly sane and rational solution to a problem that can in no other way be resolved. There can be problem resolution in a perfect world.

I can't exactly say when these thoughts first came to me, not recently, that's for sure. Ruby had nothing to do with it, not when those thoughts first arose, that is. Me, I've always had a temper…an awareness of the necessity for violence, but always kept it under control. Mom, she fucked us up. Back in Connecticut, we were taught to *"turn the other cheek"*, that everyone was God's children, and to be kind, regardless of the situation, which is a good way to raise a family of victims. The problem was that Mom forgot about the snakes and what they can do to you. I guess there's nothing wrong with turning the other cheek, but I only got one other cheek to turn. To me, that means that you give the snakes just one chance before you hit back and hit back hard. After all, fair is fair.

The first time those killing thoughts came to me was as an abstract concept. I guess when you mature, at some point, you consider what is and what is not important, what is and what is not worth fighting for, what is and what is not worth killing for, and most importantly, what is and what is not worth dying for. It would be naive to assume that there would be killing without the dying, so in that abstract sense, I guess it all came to me, many years back, that self-defense, the self-defense I never knew as a child, was the justification for killing. I figure that is no longer an abstract concept. All humans are animals and those that value their lives will survive. If it came down to it, humans can remember how to survive. Some things are worth dying for, some things are worth killing for.

**

It's something you consider back there in New York, especially in New York, coming from Connecticut. It is a violent and ruthless place, you have to consider violence and your possible reactions to it, everywhere you go. I've been told I'm "counter-phobic"...I don't like being told to avoid something, to fear something. When I am told to fear something, it seems I go out and look for it. The one thing you can hold onto when they try to take away from you, is your pride, your ability to hold your head high and to go where you please. By being safe and careful, one already is losing a degree of self-respect and freedom.

The funny thing is, there's lots of 'em back there that don't consider such things. There's a heavy layer of insulation that is shed quickly the first time they have to confront hard, cold reality. Ruby's brother Mike was a good guy, a musician that used to live mostly on coffee and cigarettes. He was in this intellectual circle and didn't really consider the animal reality of the human condition.

It wasn't until after we all got to Texas, we got the phone call about his close brush with it. It was just one of those things, one of those odds-against-it, three-in-the-morning, how-the-fuck-did-this-happen, close brush with it, but there it was...three in the morning, and there they were, out in the middle of nowhere, with no one nearby, no witnesses, their intention more than obvious, with Mike all alone, suddenly aware of the necessity of his own survival, suddenly relying on his speed and cunning he had never known he had. So there was Mike, suddenly confronting mortality, relying on his own newly-found animal reality, and getting out alive.

Back there in New York, people would brag about how many times they got mugged. Some would brag about all the adversity they'd been subjected to with this eerie kind of pride about how shitty their quality of life really was. In a great many cases, New York was an endurance contest no one ever really won. People were proud they made it through another day, with no real quality of life and then boldly would tell the story to those who would listen. Me, I couldn't go on living that way.

***

Ruby where are you tonight? Ruby what face are you wearing? I've had a part of me ripped out, chewed up, and spat out, right there in front of me. In the years that have passed, I tried to make for her a safe home, a sanctuary from that which haunts her, an understanding partner to whom she could cry. I tried, tried so hard to keep those demons out, but I didn't really know...how could I? How does anyone really know? I began to see that evil as they were, those demons made her feel at home. The terror and the fear was comforting after all those years, but I started to see it...there were two Ruby's. In lucid moments...in tears, she'd come to me and ask for help against those that hurt her. She'd ask, *"why does this happen to me?"* and wonder if it was something she had done, or was still doing that brought on all the evil, all the bad luck. Now part of me had always known that there was only so much I could do, so I couldn't tell her all at once, I had to get to her gradually. She wanted to know, but she didn't really want an answer either.

There were times I risked giving Ruby answers she insisted she wanted. In the interest of self-preservation, I always had to think about which Ruby it was I was addressing but I would try anyway.

"It ain't what comes your way, Ruby, but the way you react to it...shit happens to everyone and you're not alone. You are not alone and you gotta let some of it go!"

Ruby, well Ruby lived for the fight, there was nothing that came her way that she could let go of, and that was the other Ruby. Then the other Ruby would rear her ugly head, as I'd tell her to lighten up.

"DON'T EVER TELL ME TO LIGHTEN UP!" she'd scream, and the whole cycle would repeat itself again.

Now I don't know an awful lot of math, but I do know that there are graphs and curves that explain relationships between numbers and numbers represent facts and situations, and when you look at it, those numbers represent life and the human condition. Well me, me an' Ruby both saw things as heading toward some sort of conclusion. She knew what had happened, she knew she wasn't happy, and in those lucid moments, Ruby wanted nothing more than to throw those demons out. I remember a graph with an "X" and a "Y" axis, and a curve that runs between the two.

***

To the naked eye, that curve looks like it's reaching a point on that axis, looks like it's actually gonna touch. Well, the mathematics behind that particular equation is such that the curve gets closer and closer to that axis, but never actually reaches it. You could magnify that whole curve, look at it, and see that it still gets closer and closer, but still never touches. That curve is so close Lord, but that curve never reaches the axis. Such is the case with human behavior, and such is the case with Ruby's quest for happiness. Ruby gets closer and closer, closer and closer, she's so close she can see it, she knows where it is. Poor Ruby, though, has not reached that point, cannot reach that point, she just keeps getting closer and closer. It seems that being that close may not make any difference at all, she's just as far away from it as she's ever been. The closeness must make it all that much more painful, and with those demons driving her, they are never gonna let her come any closer to that line.

***

Graffiti to me was self-expression. People have said, *"everyone is an artist."* I guess everyone is an artist of their own design, the common thread is the desire to express oneself. It is probably a common thread throughout humankind, the inhibiting factor being the degree of "desire" to self-express over the reality of self-expression.

People get confused over "rights". Do people possess the right to self-expression? Is my right to create what I consider a work of art on someone else's wall the same as some less-talented person's right to scribble over that same piece of art? The whole scenario seems to be one of nature taking its course, and I can't really see an answer one way or the other, it's just the way things are.

"Rights" is a thing that the modern age has spoiled us into believing is an inherent truth. Here in America, here in this modern world, we have certain freedoms that we probably take for granted, but on the whole scale of things, history may prove that there are no rights, just opportunities that may or may not exist tomorrow. The things one would kill for, the things one would die for...in the cold, hard picture, we may not have a damned right to do anything. Is our own desire to self-express and to live life as we see fit, is all that we hold dear worth the ultimate sacrifice?

I used to get a kick outa seein' the spoiled skinheads drivin' in from New Jersey in mom's car. They'd come down to the Lower East Side, acting all poor and underprivileged and all, acting like they had some kinda right, sitting around drinking beer, spitting, trying to piss people off, trying to be scary, but what would they fight for, and what "rights" would they die for? They dressed like their working class counterparts, but what I saw, was carloads of spoiled suburban kids, unaccountable for their own personal actions, hiding behind the guise of personal freedom and self-expression, all the while exercising their rights. I feel that if people felt less entitled to their rights, perhaps they would enjoy their precious freedom all the more.

***

Ruby, well Ruby was self-expressive. There was that point of frustration where Ruby realized that if she broke through, she would have only herself to confront, that there would be no one else to blame. Well, being alone with herself would leave her alone and with her demons. Ruby could express thoughts about this and that, express very strong opinions about most any subject, especially those that came up right in her face, or those that planned to do her harm, but Ruby lacked ultimate self-expression. Ultimate self-expression...that point where one self-actualizes and breaks through that barrier of frustration, breaking the chains that hold one down. Ruby could self-express, but only to a point and no point further. That one point of self-expression that would break loose the bond that held her down was somewhere else, always somewhere else, and like the ideals she held so dear…far far away.

Me, I have a need for constant self-expression. It could be a result of alienation and misunderstanding as a child…hell, as an adult as well. I guess all humans are misunderstood, but I guess like Ruby, I saw myself as an island, alone and forever misunderstood. I had to start creating, painting, and to make sure the world understood me, or at least so I would understand me, I had to put it on the walls for all to see.

The world will tell you what you can and cannot do...there is always an army of assholes standing in your way of succeeding, standing in your way of self-expression. So Graffiti is great, they tell you that you can't do it, there's laws against it, cops'll break your head for doing it, citizens shun you, crews don't want you on their turf, but you go out and you do it anyway. It carries over to the rest of life...everyone's telling you not to do something...not to take chances, not to go for it, not to put yourself out on the edge, for that one shot that may work out for you, that one shot that may put you ahead of the rest, that one shot that will make others realize that they have fallen into the safe cushion of complacency, so you go out and you do it anyway…

***

So in those days, Ruby was Whiteboy's girl. She liked it too. Ludlow Street was scary in those days...maybe not completely dangerous, but the potential was always there. They sold a lotta dope down there, and there's no telling what junkies'll do. When crack became the next big thing, I was glad I lived on the block that knocked 'em out instead of the block that wound 'em up. I can see the thrill of being stimulated, but to spend 24-7 chasing after something that makes you a hundred times more nervous than a career in Advertising, fuck it...it wasn't that bad living among the junkies.

Ruby had moved to New York from Tacoma and had been a normal adult with a normal job and had her teenage daughter, Lizzie. Now I can't say Ruby was all that normal in her life, where she had lived and all, but I knew that Ruby hadn't seen anything quite like Ludlow Street, back in the early days when everything was available, but you had to cross Houston Street to buy a legal drink, and I think that was one reason we were both glad we had found one another.

Up until a point, no one knew who Whiteboy was. It was very cool being that anonymous. Someone in the building, down the hall, someone would say something about seeing all this 'Whiteboy" stuff up on the walls everywhere, and I'd just nod and smile. Every now and then, someone would be coming home from a club or some after-hours about five, six in the morning and see me rolling in, hands all covered with paint, and clothes all dirty, every molecule in my being still reeling from the fumes. It was no great claim to fame, but it was great to have that "other identity" and not have to share it with anyone else.

Coming out of the Graffiti Closet was a weird thing. I was a solo act, the Lone Ranger with spray cans, and I went out alone every night with no crew, no lookout, no partner, with no safety. No one knew who I was. Graffiti is illegal, and some get their heads busted for doing it. Some people care, and some don't, but you don't have to explain yourself to anyone. All of a sudden, the day comes, when people start realizing who you are, what you do, and boom! There you are, wondering if the cops know, wondering if the cops care. There you are in the center of everyone's attention, there you are in the center of everyone's expectations.

***

There were two Ruby's, hell there's two of all of us. That "Parallel Universe," the equal but opposite place that everyone imagines, is actually right here within each and every one of us. The Evil Twin lies within us all. We are all two, and our two sides fuse to make us one. Back in Connecticut, that other side was hidden so deeply and so feared, that for appearances, there was only one. It may not necessarily be "evil" as such, but the other side of our existence. Ruby's two sides were plain and obvious. I think she knew it, too, but when that one twin rears its ugly head, the other one refuses to recognize it. From a distance, in lucid moments, in a perfect world, even Ruby saw that tore-up tortured other self, but the human condition in all its splendor cannot allow that much conflict within one's own self. There is only room for one at a time.

Ruby's other side was the one where those demons lived. Without those demons there would've still been another side, but that was where they came in and that was where they resided. Ruby was a shining diamond in the night, brilliant and caring, but that Ruby needed to rest. That Ruby would have to slow down and let the other Ruby take over. That other Ruby was scared and tired. That other Ruby had been host to her demons for so long, that they just woke up and took over whenever they saw fit. That other Ruby was angry, angry for what had been done to her, angry that she allowed it to happen, angry that she let 'em stay for so long. That Ruby was in torment and the world was her enemy. No one could be trusted in a world that'd allow this to happen to her. Everyone was suspect. If the world allowed those demons to come in and stay like that, then they must have wanted 'em to, and since it wasn't her fault, then it was the world's fault, and they were all part of the plan, and it was a big world-wide plan that everyone was in on. That other Ruby had no use for people and what they had done to her.

***

Which Ruby I fell for could be debated, but to tell the truth I know it was both of 'em. The Ruby I first fell for, the one I hope to see again, was strong, independent, honest, loyal and true. She was an old fashion-type girl from another day, a day I remembered and longed for. Now that day I remembered was from Connecticut, and hers was from another place, but us souls can't control where we end up, and in spite of all the whitewash and such back there in New England, I think I saw right through it, I knew right from wrong, without the Puritan smoke screen.

The difference may be that I came up in the shadow of the Bomb. First day of school, back in the early 60s, they took us on a tour of the bomb shelter in the school basement. Along with the mandatory fire drills, we also had air raid drills, where we would file into the hall, and all of us young innocents would duck and cover, in case they ever dropped the Atomic Bomb. Back home, Mom still had a book from World War II that identified the underside of enemy aircraft, in case of attack. Fragile, growing six-year-old mind takes it all in with no great horror, but it's always there and it never goes away, it's just always there.

Years later, in college we were at an electric Kool Aid party...green Kool Aid... *"Think Green"* they were saying that night. I was talking to someone as Pink Floyd came on singing *"Mother Do Think They'll Drop The Bomb?"* We started talking and talking about it, and all of a sudden I realized that the other guy was talking about the Atomic Bomb while I was talking about the Neutron Bomb. After all, they had already dropped the Atomic Bomb. There were just too many bombs to keep track of. It doesn't ever go away, it's just there...it's always just there. I guess those were my demons, maybe that's why I had a connection with the other Ruby.

The other Ruby was a hard girl to figure out, she didn't come out that often. Not at first, anyway. In more lighthearted moments, I called that other girl, "Hurricane Ruby." Perhaps she would be able to see some humor and irony somewhere in all of that sad, aggressive behavior. Me, I'm an optimist so I'm usually disappointed.

***

So the other Ruby was a child, where no child had been allowed to reside. That Ruby was scared, and so scared, she carried on like a hurricane. Nothing would ever be right, so why go on trying? Some people, with all the pop culture psychology would say Ruby and me were "codependent" or some such thing, and ask why I put up with those two Ruby's. Well, I assume, bottom line, with respect to all those sad country songs, in a word the answer would be "Love". Damn I loved that girl like it was meant to be, like I knew her from the beginning of time, and I wanted to be with her throughout eternity. I wanted to see the end-of-the-world with her.

Ruby used to talk about how not all of the souls were the same since the beginning of time, that some of 'em split and sometimes they were one soul living in two bodies. I saw us as one of those souls looking to get back together.

Now this other Ruby, the problem was that I couldn't be in love with one Ruby without being in love with the other...I had this special affinity toward her. I had seen her sadness, I had been through her torture. Me, I don't think my demons put me through nearly as much, but my demons never had been kind to me, either. I had been on both sides of insanity, and I had usually seemed to come out of it okay. Well, up 'til now I suppose. Now I know everyone's different, and no two people's cure is the same, but me, if there was one helping hand back when I was going through it, it would have been appreciated. On the surface, it may only matter now, looking back on it, but it feels like it would have made things better. Ruby used to say, *"you don't know how much you really affect people, or in how many ways you may touch their lives."* See, Ruby used to believe in Karma.

***

Maybe I did touch Ruby's life, and maybe it was just my warped sense of problem resolution. Maybe I demand solutions, maybe I don't see why someone would be so self-aggravated miserable. At this point in time, I can't say, it's obvious I don't really know anything anyway. But me, I had been in the depths of despair, I had been on the edge, way out on the edge. I remember that subway train, the CC Local, rolling into the Spring Street station, dank and underground, more rats than humans. Strange faces glaring from the sides of my reality as I descended down the dark, dirty steps, down from the street level, blaring car alarms and loud honking truck horns being left behind. I remember that split second I thought to hang on, and hang on tight. I wrapped my arms around that massive I-beam, fingernails dug in as deep as I could into the cold, hard metal. I hung on for dear life as the train rumbled into the station, platform shaking with life-threatening intensity. I was the only one on the planet, and I was fighting my own worst enemy for those twelve or thirteen seconds when I almost gave up forever.

I had been there when the walls closed in, but I learned and I learned good. I learned that I had seen it. I had seen it and I loved her, and I knew what she was going through, but no, I wasn't her, I couldn't know, I could never know. Only Ruby had the key to unlock that door. I could walk her to the door, maybe I did, I mighta left her standing in front of that door for all I know, but she didn't like it there and she left for the security of her own sadness. Ruby left, and only Ruby's got the key.

Ruby said she was no good in marriage and she used that institution to blame, instead of looking at it like it was just me and just her. I told her after she left that I was just a mirror of her, a mirror of her and a mirror of her own demons, but those demons were more pronounced in the face of another, if she could only remember, but I knew she wouldn't believe that, I knew those demons were gonna be in that bed with her long after I was, long after she left. But Ruby, Ruby's gotta see that all for herself. I know what's gonna happen. Someday, long after she left, long after the last time I ever saw her troubled face, someday Ruby's gonna see her demons. One day, Ruby's gonna confront her demons.

***

So Ludlow Street, back in the days...I've always seen we were living there on the brink of disaster. Me, I've never been a prophet of doom, but growing up in the shadow of the Bomb, being raised on duck and cover, remembering that tour of the bomb shelter on Day One, I quickly saw through all that Connecticut bullshit, and saw us for the primitives we really were. Only technology evolves...the weapons became more advanced, be we're all still scared animals living in caves. Caves now, with central heat and air conditioning, indoor plumbing, manicured yards, and barbecue in the backyard, but where is the real difference? There really isn't one. We all still live in caves. We all still live in fear.

When Punk Rock first kicked in, I thought of "Road Warrior" as I used to see all these scary leather-clad mohawks, steel-toed boots, and such, and thought that maybe the next generation really was really aware of the demise. Maybe this was the generation that truly knew how close we all really were. The religious nut jobs would have thought that the Punks were the source of the demise, but me, I had seen 'em as the warriors who would survive, who would survive by seeing the necessity of survival at the end-of-the-world, but I was naive and I was wrong.

I remember early in those days, before New York, the first Punks I knew were from Boston, Boston I guess, too much like Hartford. This was the early 80's, maybe late 70's, when Carol told me about how these tough-ass jocks bust in on a party one of 'em was throwing, there in their own apartment, beat the shit outa everyone in the room. I must have seen things different, 'cause I had to ask Carol, what about the attitude, what about Armageddon? What about Road Warrior? Carol explained that these were all artists and musicians and such and were not very physical, and I just stood there, speechless. Was I the only one aware of the impending doom? Was all this Punk Rock Road Warrior bullshit merely a fashion statement? Were all these end-of-the-world Hard-Core Metal Punk Rock leather-wearing assholes really that weak and really that stupid?

Another illusion shattered, I wandered off alone to confront the demise...on to New York City.

NEW YORK CITY

New York seemed to be the best place to confront the demise. People were already on their survival wavelength, the animal within was all right there on the surface, right out in the open where the Connecticut Puritans didn't want to see it. In New York there was no shame. In New York not that many people owned cars. Very few people there had the necessity to own cars. In spite of Road Warrior, I pictured the survivors being on foot. The neighborhoods I lived in were already half destroyed, and I remember a newspaper article comparing the ruins of Harlem and the South Bronx and the Lower East Side to Dresden, Berlin, and Beirut, after the bombings, and when I picked up on the comparison, it all started making perfect sense.

Yes, New York was the place to get ready for the demise. I had left Connecticut denial behind, and confrontation was the equal and opposite reaction. There is no better time than the present to get on with things.

I arrived in New York in August of '84, not knowing a soul there, except Clive Bunker, who I really didn't care for too much anyway. Clive was a self-appreciated individual who was already dropping four-ways of Orange Sunshine back in the eighth grade, and bragged that his parents took him to "R" rated movies, but Clive Bunker grew up and became an adult, cut his hair and was now living an adult's life in New York. Clive Bunker now had his big job in Advertising...laying out the Sunday newspaper inserts, the ones with all the shopping coupons. Clive Bunker usually bragged about his sex life and those early four-ways of Orange Sunshine had become three-ways with young girls he had managed to scam along the way. He kept a journal of his dreams and had gone to all the expensive seminars and had paid large sums of money to learn how to feel good about himself. Clive Bunker had paid dearly to learn that he was the center of his own Universe. I looked him up once to say hello, but didn't stay in touch. Clive was on his own collision course and couldn't have helped me anyway...I'd rather prepare for the demise on my own. I landed in Bed-Stuy, Brooklyn, out near Pratt Institute, which seemed as good a place as any. It was the Tabula Rosa, a blank slate, my fresh start, a chance to leave Connecticut behind.

***

New York is New York, but to me it had a different perspective...a couple of hours from Leave It to Beaver, and light years away. It was so near, yet so far, and there were people I used to know, who'd take a cruise or a long-distance vacation, but would consider the two hours to New York to be too much trouble, too far away, too different. Back in high school, there were all the risk-takers, and they seemed cool as shit, but when the real world kicked in, most of those assholes either totally chickened out, or ended up in Boston. There's nothing wrong with Boston, but in defiance of the Puritanical ideals I so anxiously sought to abandon, Boston was little more than Hartford with Punks. The Mayflower landed too close to Boston for anything too extreme to happen there. Boston was safe and predictable, and that's fine for those who want it, but everything there was clearly linear. The future is a relatively clear concept in Boston. Me, I like to venture deep into the unknown. There is nothing like living in the movie without a script...it sharpens the senses, makes you ready for anything, so all the risk-takers ended up in Boston while I headed out for the unknown in New York.

***

Back in those days, I was bombing walls all over downtown, mostly in Alphabet City and on the Lower East Side, and had the run of Ludlow Street from Houston Street all the way to Chinatown. Crazy Greg from Brooklyn used to shake his head and ask me why I "looked up" to the drug dealers back there. Crazy Greg, he had his share of dope, had probably been on and off the block for many, many years prior, and it was obvious he was very glad he survived, but he only saw it in black and white, his black and white, and I guess in his post-heroin survival, that was the way he had to sort things out. Me, my survival was moving onto the block, the block which was run by the crazies with guns, the dealers, the dealers and their families, the dealers and their families who been on the block since they left Puerto Rico, many years before, and I didn't think it was gonna fly to come down from Connecticut and tell them how things should be. To me, the best way of getting by was to meet the crazies with the guns, and to make sure everything's cool. Crazy

Greg could go back to Brooklyn, and deal with his neighbors there, but me, I lived there on Dope Street, and my black and white…my survival, was not the same as Crazy Greg's.

Ludlow was my street and Ruby was my girl. Ruby was different, and Ruby was just passing through. She wanted to be a party girl again, but it didn't take her too long to realize that she couldn't just go back into her youth, and have that same reckless abandon she realized she had missed. There were too many considerations and responsibilities that anchored that free spirit. Me, I had grown sick of all the fashion queens in rehab, all those nameless faces, and it was hard to have a relationship that lasted more than a month. I was starting to think about stability. Ironically, that was when I thought my life should start getting a little more boring. I had expectations, again of approaching a new chapter of the unknown, not knowing then, that that piece of Karma was going to kick me in the ass but good.

Ruby was something else. Perhaps I shouldn't have put so much emphasis on that, but back there on the Lower East Side, Ruby was one of a kind. I was surrounded with bullshit, and I was tired of hearing about whether so-an-so should quit drinking or just kick methadone, or if she should just start adding a little speed or coke so she could make it back to work again. In those days, in that place, Ruby was a priceless find.

Does a butterfly need an anchor? Do opposites attract? I never really thought about Ruby and me as opposites. I saw us more like compliments; I used to think that a right brain and a left brain had a better chance of survival, because that combination made the thought process complete. I always thought I stood a better chance of getting by as an artist if I had an anchor to help keep my feet on the ground, to keep me sane, perhaps to make things a little bit safer. Looking back on it now, I guess that's no different than trying to take off in a boat with one foot still on the dock. The trouble is, looking back on it now, I can't ever change how I saw it then.

***

Back in those days, people were all just passing through. Everyone was on the run, and no one really got to know anyone else. People are so fucked up, they really don't wanna settle down, and most don't wanna let you in until you've already gotten attached. I used to live by the "six month" rule. You could be with someone about six months before the skeletons started coming out. There were too many secrets and too many skeletons and most of 'em just want a good fuck for the night. Sometimes that fuck was so much of a mind-blower, and sometimes you just didn't want her to leave before the morning comes. Sometimes you'd end up stuck in that situation, you'd end up just kidding yourself, and sometimes it just wasn't as significant after the fact.

Perhaps I shouldn't have dropped that night. Perhaps I shouldn't have put so much emphasis on Ruby that night. Me and Tia…Tia a beautiful specimen of Chinese womanhood and me started working on something over the past few weeks, but neither one of us was really sure where it was going. Me and Tia and Aussie Bob all dropped that night and left our futures to the winds of fate.

Significance is a funny thing. Something can be extremely significant at one particular point in time, but that significance can get lost into the future. I used to be extremely naive, born and raised in Connecticut. My naiveté still raised its ugly head, and leaving Connecticut was not as clear as turning off a light switch. Looking back on it, Ruby and me were probably destined to have one mind-warping all-night fuck, then should have said good-bye. Ruby with her changing faces made it hard to tell for sure. At that point, she hadn't slept with anyone in several years, and she was ready for her next journey. At least that's how she remembered it. Time is relative anyway, and there's no telling how long those several years really were.

***

If anything, perhaps the significance lay in the necessity of Ruby and me bending the mattress for maybe a few days, then saying good-bye and good-luck. In Connecticut however, that was fornication, it was sinful and possessed no worthwhile contribution to society, it had no significance. Down there on the Lower East Side, perhaps that's all we were meant to do.

I can't say everyone from Connecticut had the same fear I did. I was taught about sex out of necessity, and Mom used to teach "Family Life" in her high school Home Ec class. The trouble was the talk would always precede with, *"on your wedding night..."* I had always justified the act of fornication by telling the one I slept with that I "loved" her. Fornication with "love" was not really a sin. I even used to fool myself in those days. I can't really blame the Puritans, I only have myself to blame. It was a slow process, but I learned how to have good non-committal sex, but it was not without guilt. What they put in your mind when you are really young usually lays so deep, it's hard to sort out the feelings. It's hard to figure out exactly where the feelings are coming from. Sometimes they aren't even feelings. Sometimes that's just the way things were.

I should have cut Ruby loose, but I thought I had found significance in having found her. The sex was okay, not that good, but okay. When the sex started getting better, and things started getting crazy again, Ruby made sure that we would both remain in our right minds and the sex went back to being okay again. I started kidding myself into thinking that that wasn't the reason that we were together, but without sex, exactly why were we together? My mind started traveling light years ahead, thinking of all the good me and Ruby were gonna do together.

***

I remember moving to New York on the brink of humankind's demise. The world was a shitty place, and I wanted to go down and live out the Armageddon. New York was as good a place as any. Everyone was already in Survival Mode, and the animals do know how to survive.

I was born in the Fifties, when there was Cold War paranoia permeating most of all that was happening. It was not so much a conscious thing, but I remember that first day of school, young impressionable First Grade minds taken on a tour of the bomb shelter in the school basement, Fallout Shelter signs leading the way. I don't recall how far into the Second Grade this carried into, but the lingering memory of the Red Scare didn't go away when the Air Raid Drills stopped. I remembered the book Mom showed me and I used to look up to the sky, walking home from school. Looking up in the sky, watching...waiting.

I remember as a child, beginning to draw and color, I would make pictures of the End-of-the-World. Somewhere there may exist a horror movie long forgotten that actually gave me those early images of the Armageddon...I'm not sure. I vividly remember drawing smashed up haunted houses with broken windows, with black clouds and tornadoes tearing through the Earth, explosions everywhere. All this was mine…my world's view, between six and eight years old. It was not a conscious thing, but apparently since an early age, I was getting ready for the End of the World.

"The World Has Ended And You've Already Missed It."

***

Heroin is one of those things that to me, doesn't really deserve elaborate commentary. Every idiot on Ludlow Street, every idiot with an opinion, of which there were many, would go off with some philosophical discourse about "morality", "social causes" and whatever else. Chester's girlfriend used to show up, eyes half shut, bumping into the doorway, nodding out at the kitchen table, with drool on her chin, and would lay on me that I shouldn't knock it 'til I've tried it, but I've seen the dope line. I've seen Chester's girlfriend nodding out at the kitchen table and I've seen the dope line wind down Ludlow Street and back in those early days, the drama was amazing.

The store would open, and the junkies were not supposed to be on the block before the store opened, it drew too much attention to things. If the lookout was in a good mood, he'd disperse them, tell them all to leave, but on a usual day, he'd bash heads, bash heads to make a point. On a rainy day, I'd look down from my fourth floor window and see thirty to forty people casually hanging out under a sea of conspicuous umbrellas. Even at street level it was conspicuous, but from the bird's eye view, the behavior looked predictable, it looked stupid and it looked pathetic. There was almost humor in the stupidity, but it wasn't one bit funny.

The store would open at irregular intervals with no forewarning. As soon as the man with the product would show up, those who hadn't been thrown too far off the block would rush up to be first in line. Back then, when even the cops were afraid, or just not willing to deal with it, there were usually two running the store. One took the money and handled the dope, while the other stood by with a baseball bat, just to keep things honest. The junkies would not leave 'til they copped, pure and simple. The dealers knew that, everyone knew that. The dealers were shining in the Sun. There was no conscious thought about tomorrow, but deep down inside, getting paid in product and not in money, they knew it wouldn't be long until they were on the other side of the line, waiting.

***

At that time, the dealers had power over the lost souls and they knew it. If they didn't like your look, if you said something they didn't like, if you so much as reminded them of someone they didn't like, you would not score. Most of the junkies would have preferred a bat to the head for a bag of dope, but no dope was leaving a starving man without food, and they kept coming back for more. More times than not, the women would take the dealers into the stairwell of some unlocked building to trade fleeting affection for product.

Jimmy Money came down one day and told me that all the workers were getting blowjobs up on the second floor stairwell, and *"just go on in if you want one Whiteboy"*. It was nice to see Jimmy taking care of his crew in an industry that typically didn't offer workplace benefits, but I declined. The women could always score one way or the other, but the men, the men just had to take whatever shit came their way, and like Divine fate, probably like life itself, sometimes you score and sometimes you don't.

Dope is a metaphor for the grander scheme of things. New York brings it more to a vivid understanding, but it is true anywhere, there are winners and there are losers. There's really no middle ground. You either have your shit together or you don't. I used to think, but this was New York in the Eighties, I used to think that success was fame and fortune. After a while it became more apparent, that what success was, was simply surviving. I couldn't really see the pursuit of dope as survival...too much had already been lost. *The Natural State is Survival.*

***

It's only been recently, it's only been a short time in history that man forgot about survival. It is commonly perceived that man has only recently showed up in the history of the world, and in that time frame, the Industrial Revolution and the illusion of security and "success" has been around for maybe a split second. Aboriginal cultures, those in the Third World, any war-ravaged country and those lucky enough to have grown up during the Depression have a better concept of what survival really is. Growing up in Connecticut during the Sixties led me to believe that everything was gonna be just fine. I have heard some who grew up back then and back there, lament over the dissolution of that security, but it never really was there. That contrived sense of "security" only served to give us poor souls the false illusion that everything was okay and everyone was safe. Me, I never fell for it. I never really knew why I was rejecting all that sense of security, but there must have been a vision of the future, or a memory of the past...the primitive past, that helped me past the illusion that life is in fact, secure.

***

*Ruby was the bitch from Hell. Ruby was the bitch from Hell.
Testing...Ruby was the bitch from Hell.*

***

Security, I suppose I married Ruby for security, funny as it seems now. I figured that I had had my share of fun, and it was the dawn of the Plague. Running with that many, I considered myself lucky and started to count my blessings. I suppose that getting married as a form of avoidance was perhaps practical, probably not intimate, but that seeking of security, now seems ironic and somehow funny.

Ruby was an old fashioned girl, and seemed to touch a part of me that was always there on the side, a touch with the past, a sense of honesty and decency. I've had my fun, and I've run from the law, but I never stole anything and I never hurt anyone who didn't hurt me first. In New York, all that changed, and I never hurt anyone that wasn't about to hurt me first. Survival is relative and in New York survival was more like, *"Do unto others before they do unto you."*

I never knew what was gonna come next, and life was always just jumping out at me. Life was never boring, but I was starting to think that maybe it should be just a little less so. A close call with incarceration made me think it was time to move on. *"Growing up"* serves no useful purpose, and is more an illusion than not, but

"moving on" is a good way to take care of things as you go down
the road...

When I was young and rebellious, well younger and even
more rebellious, I would look at those businessmen in traffic and
wonder how someone could ever get that old. It didn't take long to
realize that they wanted to be that old. You don't really see it until
around college, but there comes a time in people's lives when they
decide that it's time to stop dropping Acid and start being a
responsible citizen, for some strange reason or another. Part of the
transformation is intentional, and part of it is consequential. Buying
suits, growing a mustache, smoking a pipe and driving the family
station wagon, mini-van, whatever…is all part of the great cultural
buy-in...losing your hair, buying ulcers and such, is a true benefit
toward reaching that golden maturity they all strive so hard to
achieve.

***

I never understood people who needed to grow up. There's
those that can't wait to grow up, because of an inability to endure
childhood trauma. Everyone goes through it, through no fault of
their own. Kids, especially boys, get beat up, and such, which is all
a part of growing up. It's a sad part of growing up, but it's a part of
our connection with the animals...the pecking order is established.
Although humans think they are so far above the "lesser species", as
is true in all species, big eats small. There is a sadness in the weak
being eaten, but humankind's warped progression has convinced
everyone that this will not occur to the human animal. There exists a
larger danger in the evolution of the weak and defeated into what
they will later become. There is nothing wrong with the weak or

defeated, but they strive so hard to grow up, they strive so hard to seek out revenge, they scare the hell out of me.

You can seem them in society, certain teachers, managers and bosses at your job...people who serve no other purpose in life than to make everyone else's existence pure hell. Back in Connecticut, there was this kid, a pure geek, which by itself wouldn't have been that bad, but there were glimpses of bizarre behavior even at an early age. Tim Lippincott was physically ugly...had no manners nor social skills, and basically was a rude and selfish individual. Tim really shouldn't have gotten all the abuse, he probably should have just been left alone.

Tim used to patrol the perimeter of his parent's yard with a BB gun, this at 17 years old, to me a deadly warning sign. Tim eventually got into the Police Auxiliary in nearby Windon, Connecticut. Well, eighteen rolled around and Tim decided it was time to grow up, that it was time to become a man, so Tim up and joined the Marine Corps. Within a month, Tim got thrown out on an "Undesirable Discharge," and within two months after that, Tim went back to Windon, Connecticut into the Police Academy, and to this day, Tim Lippincott is a police officer in Windon, Connecticut. Tim Lippincott was a time bomb just waiting to grow up, and grow up he did.

***

There was something inside me that wanted to grow up. Ludlow Street was becoming a dead end and even without addiction, I could see now that the dope line was a symbol all along of that dead end I was confronting. The Plague was everywhere and new diseases seemed to appear at a whim. New York had hit its peak, which to me represented the decline of the nation, the decline of the world, and the decline of Humanity. There was rich and there was poor, we had hit a Depression and no one, not the politicians, not the media, no fuckin' body, but us poor slobs dared even mention that fact. Banks and financial institutions were going belly up. Factories were closing up or moving to Mexico or wherever, and shit was shit. Perhaps I should have moved on and got over it, but no, I decided that it was time to grow up.

Karma works in funny ways. No, actually Karma only works in one way, it's just manifested in ironic situations. From afar, there is perfect symmetry in its clarity, but when you are deep in the middle of it, Karma can be a stranger in a long, black car.

***

Getting married was no big deal. As a matter of fact, getting married seemed to be the only thing to do. Living together was never a valid option. All of the inconvenience and lack of privacy that people equate with marriage is equally present in cohabitation, so I figured either to do it or not…why not do it right, and go all the way? Mom used to think we were in agreement about cohabitation until I told her why I disapproved of it. Mom just thought it was immoral, and it was an easy way out for guys who wanted sex but wouldn't commit to a woman. *"Getting the milk for free instead of buying the cow"* was a cliché that too much equated value-for-value and I'm not sure if the married daughter of Puritans even considered what *"buying the cow"* really meant. I just found the whole thing inconvenient. Marriage was Ruby's idea, but it was only her idea because I wouldn't live together with her or any woman. I was only gonna be single or I was only gonna be married. In my mind I figured that waiting thirty-five years for the right one to come along gave me some claim to being mature enough to make the right decision.

Ruby was a shining diamond in the night, but Ruby had her demons, and needed to be saved, and me, I was gonna save her. All anyone really wants in this life is to be happy, an' if it's me that's gonna show her how that can be done, then there's nothing that can stop us, there's nothing that can get in the way. All Ruby needed was to be happy.

SECTION 2
THE ROMANCE

Ruby was an old fashioned kinda gal, and me, I was born in the Fifties in the shadow of the Bomb. My parents were from the Depression and World War II. My parents were middle class from another time. Me, I had tuned in, turned on, dropped out, dropped back in, lit up, got tattooed and seen my reflection between the lines on the mirror. The modern age is funny, I never could tell if I was indecisive or just out of place. I was somewhere between two worlds, as the times changed all around me. The middle class values, that old-fashioned sense of things may have left me a comfort zone, when I went too far off the deep end. Whenever I'd go too far, I'd enjoy the security of having that other place to go back to.

In terms of substances, I guess my background showed me that sobriety was the natural state. Substances, ingredients, whatever, were the icing, substances were the dessert, but you can't keep eating all that ice cream your whole life, day after day. I never could quite see what it was about that that people didn't or couldn't understand. The politically correct phrase that people use these days is *"addictive personality"*, but I don't know what that really means. I guess there's always been those that can't handle their stuff, but this modern age, this separation from our animal selves, this separation from our ability to survive on our own has just fucked things up badly. We have the political correctness, we have the correct phrases, we have the compassion to create the victims and then fix the victims, and the cycle continues…none of which I really understand.

You could witness it in other people's behavior, it's not too hard to draw conclusions. *"If all your friends were drinking poison, would you do it too?"* Shades of common sense from the other generation. I'm probably lucky I'm not addictive, life is for savoring and life is for tasting. I have thanked the Spirit that I have had the ability to taste and to savor. The women, the substances, the food and the drink along the way have made it all worth living.

***

Crazy Carla was this insane Mexican-Puerto Rican nymphomaniac I hung with my last two weeks of college. She was eighteen, a freshman, and ready to taste everything there was to taste. We smoked, ate Peyote, drank too much, and fucked like it was the end-of-the-world. Her folks were wealthy and we went to stay at their impressive house down in that well-to-do corner of Connecticut just outside of New York. Crazy Carla was not exactly a Connecticut girl as I had become accustomed to, and her warm-blooded heritage burned a hole right through the sheets and left me always gasping for breath. Her father Pedro, seemed to be an all right sort at first, a successful businessman, a proud Puerto Rican father, proud of his family, proud of his daughter.

That night we drove up, we were both pretty stoned and all the lights in the house were out. I shut off the engine, and we got out of the car, shut the door, and walked up to the back door. Her mother, a former beauty queen from south of the border, greeted us in a short, see-through teddy. While Carla was getting her bag out of the car, her mother, also named Carla, hooked her arms under mine, embraced me warmly while sliding her knee gently between my legs, and smiled up at my face. I figured that maybe we had just interrupted her and Pedro's sweet reverie and didn't try to think about it too much, but for the rest of the weekend, I just couldn't keep my eyes off her, Carla's mother, beautiful, brown and warm.

Carla's parents were not like Connecticut parents I had met before. At dinner they talked about getting high and goofing on waiters when they went out. I was pretty blasted most of that weekend and didn't comment, but I listened and I thought about how open-minded they were. Carla spent the rest of the weekend sneaking into the guest bedroom and keeping me awake for hours at a time. When I finally did fall asleep, sore and exhausted, it wasn't long before she'd sneak in and wake me up again, gracefully sliding up and down on top of me, back arched, head thrown back as her long, jet black hair swayed from side to side, as my eyes slowly opened, waking up to Heaven in Connecticut.

Mornings were interesting and surreal that weekend, and her folks couldn't figure out why I was so late to breakfast every day. I could have told them to stop sending Carla in to wake me up, but that wasn't in my best interest at that time. By the time the weekend was winding down, I was in such pain, in such pure agony, that sleeping face down was pretty much impossible. To give it a rest, I adjusted by sleeping on my back, that also left me defenseless to Carla's increasing desire.

Carla's folks seemed pretty cool, but I still couldn't picture parents who allowed their eighteen-year-old daughter to fuck around so much, right under their roof, right there in front of them. I didn't want to think too much about it…the liquor and Peyote haze only made the sex that much more a part of the weekend.

About a year later, I heard that a dubious acquaintance from college, Leonard Sanchez, had been seeing Carla and spent a weekend with her at her folk's place. Leonard was of Cuban decent and shared a similar language and culture to Pedro, who had emigrated from Puerto Rico. Leonard and Pedro probably shared more in common than Pedro and I ever did. I learned that the old man found out that Carla had been sneaking into the guest bedroom with Leonard, and threw a stark-raving fit. Pedro beat the holy living shit out of Leonard and threw him unceremoniously out of the house, with nowhere to go, just a long walk to the train station with a bloodied nose and two black eyes. One year later and much out of danger, I sensed no fear, but let out a deep sigh of relief, realizing how lucky I really was during my short time spent there with Carla.

***

I have never really belonged and I'm pretty sure that I never really wanted to. I distrust belonging and I distrust belongers, and have since childhood. I'll never be a Young Republican or a Gangsta any more than I ever was a Boy Scout. Lack of belonging pushed me further out of society. All of society is based on belonging and I've always been an outsider, even in groups of rebels. People are born alone, and people die alone, and the reason people work so hard to deny that fact is far beyond me.

I dunno, when you're not a joiner, sometimes it seems that there is something on the horizon, a group perhaps. Maybe it was just me, but there always seemed to be the *non-joiners* who somehow gravitated together, I guess into a group. I was curious about what a bunch of these outcasts would be like together and how they would get along. Whenever I was able to get anywhere near the gathering of rebels, I couldn't get away fast enough. There was always a dominant male gorilla and the usual pecking order, and sometimes the female hangers-on, to complete the pack. The majority of a group of rebels, like any other group, consists of leaders and consists of followers. *Lead, swallow or get outa the way*, but that's the way it is.

Back on the Bowery, in front of the CBGB's Hardcore Matinee, all the skinheads, mohawks, weirdos and freaks were hanging out on the sidewalk. New York was a lawless pit in those days, but everyone still had to be cool to keep from going totally over the edge. Most of those skinheads in those days weren't Nazis or racist or anything other than just bored and jaded, some working class, some better-off. So anyway, the extreme of the subculture was all hanging out and when the matinee was over, and everyone started heading elsewhere, I remember watching one of the skinheads as he went around the corner, down Third Street and came back to pick up his crew, in Mom's car, a brand new Chevy Suburban with Jersey plates. The rebels, the fucking outcasts, the "non-joiners" in the brand new Chevy Suburban with Jersey plates, now going home to the safe and secure suburbs. *"Spoiled Skinheads From Jersey in Mom's Car."* It sucked.

***

Other things happened that year, I lost count of all the women, and the Plague was fast catching up. I was counting my blessings. I figured that I'd pushed it far enough, and I was grateful that I had so many fond memories with a minimum of scars. The women were crazy. Now me, I took more than a few chances. Back there in the late Eighties, I saw the Plague and I figured that it was only a matter of time before the risk would spread closer to some of those I was spending time with. The risk was less for a straight man, the risk was less for me, but the women were crazy. I remember the one who yanked a rubber from my hand, threw it across the room, angry, and told me to fuck her anyway. It was stupid and it was dangerous, but I wasn't in a state of mind to disobey an angry and horny woman.

When I once told an ex, one drunken night when we were reminiscing, that we should be "safe" because of the times, and how they had changed, she looked at me, disgusted, and said *"what kind of girls are YOU sleeping with?"* The risk was far less for me, but I didn't want to catch her stupidity, so I just up and left her laying there, ready but confused. People were dropping left and right in New York, if not from one thing, then from another.

I have my fond memories, I have no regrets, and I am eternally grateful that I escaped relatively unscathed. There were close calls, perhaps closer than I will ever realize. The Plague brought the end-of-the-world closer than it had ever been before. I started seriously thinking about settling down.

New York is a good place to not settle down. New York is a big small town, a big hometown. You feel comfortable, you could spend your whole life there. I dunno if it's because I wasn't born there, but I never had that feeling of being completely settled. Maybe it's like joining. The thing that probably keeps most people from hooking up there for good, is that no two people in that entire motherfucker have any semblance of a similar point of view.

One-night stands were too anonymous, too severe, too drunken and just too contrary to having a good time. I felt that two-night stands were a much better way of getting to know a stranger you'd never see again. If you finally broke the ice with a platonic partner, it gave you that much more to remember. All in all, it's usually better the second time. The second time, you lose about one degree of mystery, but replace it with three hundred and sixty degrees of technique and understanding that comes from a brief glimpse of familiarity. In spite of the virtues of the two-night stand, New York girls, most of 'em panicked at the thought of a second encounter. There is, or was back in those days, a horrible fear that continuity might lead to intimacy, closeness and expectations. You could have given a girl back then an engagement ring as easy as to try for a second go-round, but she would fuck your holy livin' lights out that first and only night, under the safe veil of anonymity.

***

I slept with Debbie that one night back in Brooklyn. Lance gave her to me for my birthday. Lance was supposed to help get her back to her Upper East Side apartment, but drunkenly, going over the bridge, Lance told Debbie that he was too smashed to bring her back home. As the cab rolled up in front of my place, Lance smiled, watching Debbie get outa the car and leaned over and whispered in my ear, *"Happy Birthday!"* I knew Debbie for a few years at that point, but at this time, we were both unattached and available.

Lance had known Debbie for quite a while, and he knew it would be easy. Opportunity was the direct result of proximity. It was to be a brief and somewhat awkward encounter, but me, I wanted one more, and I always wanted one more, the one to remember, before we went back to our usual uneasy semi-conscious normalities. I had no real desire to go any further than perhaps one sober, just to feel what was happening, fuck, and then back to being friends again. It's worked before and it's worked since. I had a breakfast date showing up that morning and didn't really need any more complications than one more fuck. Just one more, a quick one, before the next one showed up. I may as well have dumped a bucket of ice all over her reality, talk about cold! She was positive that repetition would lead to love, marriage and children. I just wanted one more as a warm-up for my breakfast date. I have since learned that sobriety and meaningless behavior do not mix.

***

I was getting tired. I had survived the Eighties in New York without too much serious damage, nor the need to enter rehab. I was getting too old to dodge the cops, coat pockets rattling with the too many spray cans I used to carry. Lungs full of colors, alone, late night, early morning in that aged tenement, faces starin' back at me from that ancient cracked plaster ceiling was becoming all too familiar. Alone was really alone, cold was really cold. I was gettin' tired. And something had to change.

Ruby was from another time and another place. I was thinking more and more that Ruby would bring me back to that place, that place safe and quiet, that place where people didn't have ulterior motives, that place where you could just live and love and be left alone.

The Cafe twinkled under the infinite sky that danced colorfully around me. Ruby came in and sat down next to me, and ordered a drink. She was dressed in a beautiful creation I later learned she made herself, a lovely green satin cocktail dress. She was not dressed like the trendy Lower East Side joiners, *same shit different mohawk.* My pulse quickened with eyes dancing in the shadows. Ruby was a shining diamond in the night. Ruby was the one I had been waiting for. Ruby was the one.

***

Ruby didn't warm up right away, she said that trust had to be earned. She said that no one, especially no man was to be trusted, and a lot of initiation had to take place. Ruby always kept control. The big contradiction was sex. Ruby loved sex but there was vulnerability during sex, there was exposure, disclosure, and no place to hide, so Ruby liked it with the lights off. She could be a wild animal with the lights off, but call out her name, turn on the lights, or do anything that brought reality back to her, and Ruby's walls went up.

We were hitting it off pretty good, and I figured there was nothing wrong with us seeing more of each other, nothing wrong with growing accustomed to each other. It was time Ruby learned she could trust me. I was a good person and I never killed anybody. I had nothing to hide, so it was her time to learn, it was her time to learn that I was the one who could be trusted.

Ruby needed me whether she knew it or not. Ruby needed to be held and protected, she needed the one man who could be trusted, and I was gonna giver her that, give her that solidity her Daddy took away from her. I had been waiting a long time for love, and Ruby was the one I had been waiting for. After that many years, it must have been her I was waiting for.

Ruby and me hung pretty steady back then. It took a while but once she stopped trying to leave all the time, and realized I wasn't gonna let her leave anyway, then she started coming around. She started seeing things my way, and she came over to see me more and more, and started inviting me over to her place.

Back then, even before I met her, I had seen her loneliness. I looked across the street from up on my roof back there on Ludlow Street. I had seen her sad face in that darkened room, glowing blue from that portable black and white teevee that was her only companion. I later learned her brother lived right across the street from her but didn't see her, not even on Christmas, her first time in New York. I had seen Ruby's sadness and there was no confusion. Everyone wants to be happy, right? All that people need is the right person, the one who can make them smile, the one who can make them laugh. All someone needs is the one person who cares, the one they were deprived of, all those painful years of their life, a lifetime of sadness that can be erased by true and caring love. Those demons ain't immortal, those demons can be killed. Those demons, I had seen them, are as vulnerable and as mortal as any living person is. Those demons weren't anything more than mirrors, and therefore were no stronger than the people they lived in.

I'm lucky I guess. Back in Connecticut, there were no demons, none that were acknowledged at least. In Connecticut, in the proud Puritan legacy, there were ghost stories that went back to the Colonial times, ghost stories and tales of witch-hunts, but they were always history, they were always abstractions far, far away.

***

Ruby had cultures, spiritual cultures she respected and revered, times and places she held most sacred. I was glad to have found a woman so spiritual. Me, I had a deep respect for American Indian culture, and Ruby was deep into the Aboriginals of Australia. We had our spiritual bond. I had finally found a fellow believer. At that time I was probably more Agnostic than anything, but had strong leanings toward the Spirit yet unseen.

To Ruby, perfect culture, spiritual oneness, agreeable men and undamaged women were always far away, in cultures yet unspoiled. Ruby knew there were cultures somewhere else where things weren't fucked up yet. Ruby knew there was a place she would fit in and be understood. Somewhere was that place where she would be appreciated for her honesty and her true goodness. That place was somewhere else, though. That place was far, far away. That place wasn't here.

Puritan culture, I guess was my family's legacy. My great-grandfather preached at the same church where Jonathan Edwards once preached *"Sinners in the Hands of an Angry God."* Me, I had no interest in history, perhaps because of the repressive culture that that history brought to Connecticut in that modern age. If anyone had had any fun it was not discussed. No one that I knew of had to get married, but young girls were sometimes sent away with no explanation, with no further discussion. Proper people didn't drink, but everyone really did. When weed came around, some teachers and some of the younger parents were smoking it. My Mother wanted me to marry a "nice girl" from church who sewed her own clothes. Mom would go on about what a nice personality this girl had, all the while avoiding the fact that we had nothing in common. Mom knew this was a nice girl who wouldn't put-out and therefore would keep her first-born's virtue intact. Mom would call me down in New York early on a Sunday morning and ask if I had been to church that morning. I hadn't been to church since I was old enough to realize it wasn't mandatory, and she knew that, but I would answer, *"yeah, sure Mom, church..."* as I fumbled around, trying to remember how to work the coffee maker.

***

Things were crazy in those days. You never really saw the true beauty of Ludlow Street until the Sun was comin' up and the lines were runnin' out. There'd be about four or five empty forties in paper bags laying around the doorstep as the magic night glow gave way to the rising Sun sneaking up over the tenement rooftops. In those days, the world was flat and dropped off somewhere after Norfolk Street. There was nothing past the East River and the Sun rose somewhere between there and Ludlow. The tooth grinding usually stopped after the third forty and things started getting mellow by then. Hanging with some of the guys on those all-nighters, I'll never forget Chas Lee.

I met Chas Lee through Jimmy Money, as he preferred to be called. Jimmy Money was nuts, stone col' fuckin' crazy, and gettin' dusted every night made sure he stayed that way. Dope dealers were funny that way. They sold the dope, knowing that the cycle would keep going on and on, that the money would keep coming in. They knew their money came from getting people hooked, so they knew enough to stay off it. They had all this money, and they'd use the dope money, turn around and bring dust back to the crib. Dust in New York wasn't even PCP, it was ghetto-poor Formaldehyde sprayed on mint leaves and sold in tiny plastic bags. These crazy fuckers spent most of their spare time smoking embalming fluid. That shit had a nasty chemical smell. One night, one of the homies handed me a burning stick as I was coming outa the crib, walking out onto the street. At that point I didn't smoke much any more, but started to pull a drag, just to be sociable. Now that chemical burn just wisped up my nose, the early warning made me stop real quick. I stopped and politely handed it back. Early warning is better than no warning. I knew motherfuckers who got seriously dusted and would walk all the way to 42nd Street and back without even realizing it. Dust was just crazy ass shit I had no use for an' watchin' these guys an' how they were over time, made me glad I stayed away like I did.

***

I had an Old Schooler from upstate who wanted to get hooked up. He used to be a big time coke freak 'til his connection dried up. Connection used to be big time heavy, owned a business, a few houses, had a wife and a girlfriend. Freebase was big back in the Disco days, after people got tired of all the nosebleeds and surgeries. Connec used to wheel and deal and smoke. He smoked so much and liked smoking so much, he started to lose interest in things and he started to lose things. Over time Connec lost his business, his houses, one-by-one…his wife and his kids. His girlfriend went down with him, and as long as he had product, he had her. He ended up living in a crack house in Jersey City, hanging on the windows, pistol in one hand, curtains in the other. Connec knew they were out there, Connec was ready for 'em. He knew who they were and he knew what they wanted. Connec knew the CIA was behind it all, and he knew that they knew who he was and where he was at all times.

Tim was one of those rare individuals who could take it or leave it, shit he'd give it away. Tim would give it away, just to have someone to sit up and talk with all night. Tim would go to work the next day, and may or may not have some for lunch, but throughout the whole thing, he never lost his shit. Tim has cooled out since, living back upstate with his wife and kid, keeping a nice house and running a successful business. Not everyone who has been that deep in it got out unscathed, but Tim, he's a survivor. From the first days when we first met, I knew that no matter how far he went in any direction, Tim would end up on his feet.

Around that time I was down and out, Tim was gonna do one last deal, and let me run the middle for him. Things were so crazy downtown, and the Law had so much on its hands, the only way we could get snagged was by accident. Sometimes cops kicked in the wrong door at the wrong time, but this was kid stuff, risk-free, one time easy in, easy out. There was so much going on out there in the open, dope lines running down the street, a discreet deal on the side behind closed doors wouldn't draw any attention. That dope was bad shit, bad Karma, but this was a step away from that, or so I told myself. Tying up the middle, Jimmy Money put me in touch with Chas Lee.

***

Chas Lee was one cool motherfucker. Chas was like a long lost brother, a black brother grew up in East Harlem, then to the Lower East Side where his aunt thought it would be safer. It was a weird connection, Chas and me, me his brother. Somehow I had been displaced in Connecticut, but somehow years later, miles away, we met and we clicked.

Chas was an artist who did some cool-as-shit drawings and painted jackets. Chas was a Kung Fu master with full control over his body and his weapons. Chas killed a man once but never really talked about it. The story came out in pieces over time. It was nothing he was proud of or was not proud of, it was just something that happened out of necessity. Dusted-out lunatic came at him out of nowhere with a butcher knife, probably hadn't slept in days. Chas was the one left standing, with that same knife now bloodied, in his hands. Chas could slip through a crowd, work his way out of any jam and end up last man standing it was like magic. Somewhere between getting handcuffed, put in the back seat, and booked, he managed to eat, snort and stash everything, so when they finally got him to the station, they had to let him go for lack of evidence. The only thing I could see wrong with Chas was that he spent all of his creative energies, all of his experience and all of his talents, all of his life, on the pursuit of one thing. Chas Lee focused all his energy and abilities on one thing, the pursuit of cocaine. Chas Lee was never going to be the poster boy for "Just Say No". He had everything going for him except for his one single weakness.

Chas was cool, Chas maintained, Chas was always in control, except those few times I had seen him without product, coming down days later, but you gotta come down sometime. Chas had a summer home. The times when Chas wasn't on the block, you could find him at his second place, his home away from home, out at Riker's Island. Every now and then, not too often, but every now and then, Chas let his guard down and just wasn't watching his back.

So Chas ran for me while I was taking care of the middle. Chas was never short on product and could always account for all the cash. Even when Chas was needy, he knew he was being taken care of, so perhaps I was buying his honesty, but from what I had been through with Chas, I couldn't say one bad word about him. Coked as he was, I trusted Chas Lee with my life.

***

I can't really say if Chas Lee was wasting his life away. Chas had so much potential, but me, as an outsider, the Whiteboy from Connecticut, could easily say that. I could have judged, analyzed, sympathized and everything else that would have made not one bit of difference, but in his own environment, Chas Lee was probably as evolved as he was going to get. He did the best he could with what he had and Spiritually, Chas was light years ahead of most, but his weakness, his weakness kept him from being what he could have been here on this material plane. How far could he have gone? Growing up in East Harlem during the Fifties and Sixties with nowhere safe to go, when his aunt took him down to the Lower East Side, the safest place she could afford to live. In that time, at that place, Chas Lee was all he was gonna be. There wasn't anything wrong with it, but I just started looking forward to those times he'd get sent up. When Chas Lee went to his summer place, he blossomed into some of what he could have been. Months-to-a-year off the block, three squares a day, weight room, and no coke, no dope...the funny thing was that anyone could score in Rikers, Chas just chose not to. Chas had control when he was in the joint, Chas could leave his weakness back on the block. Even Chas knew when it was finally time to put the screws on his weakness and get strong again.

As soon as Chas got out...sadly, as soon as Chas got out, it usually took him less than a month to lose all the prison muscle, go back on the pipe, stop eating and stay up, usually three days at a time before he'd crash and start it up all over again. Chas and me would hang out, but I wouldn't let him smoke in my place. I wouldn't let him smoke unless he was already back on it, which usually didn't take too long, but Chas Lee was two people in one body, and even the body changed. Once he was back on the pipe though, no self-righteous, empathetic bullshit from me was ever gonna change anything.

One day, we were going over some Martial Arts stuff up in my crib, light sparring and such, and Chas, Chas went into the kitchen for a stem and came back, and threw a badass kick square to my cheek, and quick as lightening, pulled back, and all I felt was the controlled breeze of that kick, off my face. It was like the sole of his foot kissed my cheek in a hurricane of controlled fury. I saw how much control he had when he was that much outa control, I could only imagine his potential if his life weren't so much controlled by his weakness.

I always trusted Chas Lee and I always trusted Chas with Ruby. The thing about Chas was, like a lotta smokers, Chas didn't sleep much until he had to. Chas stayed up two, sometimes three days at a time. When you had a loved one coming home late at night, through the thick of the Lower East Side hookers, junkies, muggers and low life's, it was nice to know there was someone keeping a concerned eye out.

***

So the way things were in those days, nothing seemed too particularly weird. I could still tell right from wrong, good from bad. I never felt my moral imperative slip, but in terms of the behavior that surrounded me, in terms of other people's behavior, fuck it, nothing really surprised me, which is probably why Ruby seemed so normal to me.

Ruby was from another time. Ruby lamented that things had gone to shit, we had all fallen from Grace, and the final insult was that no one cared any more. Things should have been simpler, people should have known right from wrong, and people should have just treated each other right. Most of all, most of all, people should leave the children alone, and people, actually men, the way Ruby described it, men should respect womanhood.

Woman was a slave to man, and man would abuse even his own children, which was why the world was such a fucked-up place. Crawling up from the bottom, Ruby knew this, and there was no one better than her to clean up the mess. I respected her determination. Most people didn't have the time to even think about such things, let alone try to clean 'em up and make 'em better. Ruby was gonna save those that couldn't be saved, the way someone should have been there to help save Ruby when she had been alone and defenseless.

***

We seemed like the right combination, Ruby an' me. Ruby with her courageous sense of right and wrong, me with everything I'd done, everyone I'd known, strong with a moral imperative that would make things all right. Me and Ruby were gonna help people, and me and Ruby was gonna make things right.

***

My roommate Chester had this junkie asshole he used to run an after-hours with. Chester brought this guy home one day, and soon after they left I started noticing the things that were missing. Chester was more trusting than I was and most of Chester's friends were junkies. I don't like being ripped-off and I looked for this guy everywhere I went and I knew I would find him. New York is a big small town.

Out west, back on our post-college road trip, I asked Manny Wright, my traveling partner, how they used to *"head someone off at the pass."* We were out in the middle of no-fucking-where in the Arizona desert somewhere, and I couldn't quite see how you could have trailed anyone back there. I asked Manny how anyone could have found anyone out there and he responded, quite simply, *"water."* People needed water, so anyone in the wasteland had to take certain routes to find water for their journey. So it is with junkies. You can find a junkie as he heads for the next oasis in the desert. I knew I would have to find Junkie at one of his oases, in his never-ending search for water or whatever it was that kept him alive.

Some time had passed and I finally found Junkie one night down on Eleventh Street, walking with another, headed east, toward the next oasis. I quickly approached him, but he looked up and saw me. The first thing two junkies do when they realize something is about to happen, is they split up in two different directions. *Junkie Loyalty.* It didn't take long and I found Junkie cowering in a basement stairwell, below the sidewalk. I looked down, as he looked up at me and not missing a beat he said,

"Dave! I been looking for you!"

Bullshit. I dragged him by the shirt collar back toward the bar on Second Avenue. Karmically, several others he had ripped off were all inside the bar drinking and I decided to bring them all, this human offering. As he twitched and struggled, we headed east toward the bar, I firmly directed him where we were going.

"Let go of me, let go, I'll come along!"

Bullshit again, and we stopped on the curb in front of the red light. He twitched and squirmed, insisting that there was no reason to be forceful, he had nowhere to run to.

I looked out of the corner of my eyes, and when the light changed up on Twelfth Street, I counted to three and released Junkie, except for a loose hold on his shirt collar, and pushed him forcefully toward the line of oncoming, speeding, and carnivorous taxis. Junkie stumbled and panicked as I pulled him back by his collar. He regained his footing to the best of his wasted ability as the first taxi sped by, inches in front of him. He stood there stunned and panting like an animal, facing the traffic light.

"Do you still want me to let go of you?" I asked.

" N-No," he gasped, breathing rapidly, "No, I-I'll go along!"

I got the group outside of the bar, and we all shook Junkie down, going through his pockets. It wasn't likely he had anything of value, but we wanted to mitigate our collective loss some way or the other. A small, ten-dollar bag fell out of his pocket, an' Junkie, not missing a beat, lied to the best of his ability.

"I dunno what that is, that's not mine, I'm on Methadone now!"

Not that anyone was really listening anyway.

An intoxicated, older Puerto Rican man stumbled onto the scene a few minutes into it, and looking Junkie up and down, took out his wallet. He took out a fifty-dollar bill, and offered it to us. *"It couldn't be that bad, here I take care of it!"* he said, as he pushed the money toward the group. We looked at Junkie and looked at the man. Conscience wouldn't allow us to sell Junkie to this man, but not for his protection. *"No," I responded. "You don't want this one, he's bad news."* The man put the money back in his wallet, thanked us, and stumbled back up the avenue.

***

Ronald, back in Connecticut, never left the farm, even past his thirtieth birthday, told me I was sick, sick and violent.

In New York, it was swimming with sharks, running amid animals, the sharks smelt blood and the animals smelt fear. The animals would tear you to shreds, just 'cause they knew they could. In New York, especially down on the Lower East Side, swimming with the junkies, "self-defense" was a different concept. Down there, self-defense was whatever it took to keep the animals away from you, pure and simple.

Ronald, when he found out about Junkie, proceeded to tell me how good he was, an' how he helped an old lady across the street last week, and what was wrong with me anyway? He told me he went to church and did community service, and I wouldn't have shit like Junkie happen to me, if I hadn't left the farm. Helping an old lady across the street was such a cliché, but how can you argue with shit like that? I thought he was making it up, but he wasn't. Ronald was really intent on buying his way into Heaven by helping little old ladies. It was then I realized how far I had really come from Connecticut.

Life really isn't worth living without the risk. Taking chances and confronting danger add the spice to life. Nothing should be avoided, and coming to the aid of others, righting wrongs, is something you shouldn't have to think twice about. Your life ain't worth living if you're gonna live in fear or avoidance.

Being told I was counter-phobic made perfect sense to me. If someone told me to avoid something, to stay out of someplace, not to walk down Pitt Street after dark, guess where it would end up? There's no problem, just don't tell me what not to do, don't tell me that I've got to fear anything.

***

Being counter-phobic must have had something to do with all the walls I bombed back there in New York. There's physical fear, and then there's the fear that permeates the human condition in this modern world. On a different level than physical fear, there's people that all your life are telling you what you should do and how you should do it. Graffiti, there are cops who hate it so much, they'll gladly bust heads to reinforce the status quo. Not only do they tell you that you can't do it, they add the physical fear to keep you from doing it, so you do it anyway. I've noticed that when it's time to really take a chance, that when that ship is coming in and you can see it on the horizon, when you know it's really time to take your shot and go for it, go for what may be the one chance in your life to really do something, inevitably it's your closest friends and your family that will give all the reasons not to.

People will say they're looking out for your well-being, and that all they really wanna do is get you to look at the whole picture, to make sure you're not fucking up by taking that chance. People will say it's for your own good that you listen to 'em, all the while, telling you what you should and should not do. I have found that in this life, in a world full of perfect strangers, when you find the ones you can trust, those are the ones, those are the ones…more than family and friends, who will support your decision. For some reason, it's those other people in your life that will support your decision to follow that path, to follow your heart, more than those that are closest to you. The friends and the family don't want you to be disappointed when you fail.

***

Growing up in a good Christian Leave It To Beaver family in Connecticut, the first thing I remember in my upbringing was being told to deny my instincts. I guess it was figured back then that instincts were for animals and Aboriginals, and God gave us the Bible to find our course, and the voices from within were not to be listened to. That was what separated us from the animals. You weren't supposed to enjoy yourself, you weren't supposed to listen to your voices, and you sure as hell weren't supposed to rely on your own judgment.

Fortunately, the sex drive is more powerful than reason, more powerful than Christian guilt, and I remember seeing all those years of Leave It To Beaver go away in one long teenaged evening. Mom and Dad were at choir rehearsal and the time was right. She was from Oklahoma, not too pretty, kinda heavy, and one day, not too discreetly told me that she was on the Pill. Everyone back there in my hometown knew everyone else in my hometown and had all gone from K through 12 together. It wasn't too likely I was gonna score in the inner circle, and truth to tell, in that small town with no secrets, perhaps no one else was either.

There was very little lust, there was no passion. It was contrived and mechanical, and achieved the desired result. Most of the time I pulled back a bit, looked down, looked up at her, looked back down again, and incredulously took it all in. It had all been explained to me a long time ago, Dad embarrassed me with that first "talk" when I was ten or so, but it was all negated by my Mother as being a sacrament that only married couples enjoyed.

I lay there, overwhelmed in the aftermath, after she had gone back home. Reason and my upbringing started slowly working their way back into my newly liberated thoughts. I started to wonder if God or Jesus, I started to wonder if even my dead Grandfather were all up in Heaven, looking down, disapprovingly, of course. It was funny though, unlike earlier indiscretions, unlike earlier sex acts performed alone, this time the guilt didn't last.

It took a long time, it took a lot of ups and downs, and a lot of hard lessons before I realized that those voices inside of me was really God talking. Aboriginals all over the world followed their gut, listened to those voices, and followed their dream. Finally, finally in that latter part of the Twentieth Century, I started to learn to follow mine

.

***

I think it's easier to be Spiritual when you have nothing. Some people have so much their whole lives long that they can't imagine that anything's missing. They live for their possessions, they buy and sell, and if it can't be bought or sold, it ain't worth having.

I figure you have what you have, pure and simple, but it's the quality of life that matters, the quality of that which you can't buy or sell. You walk through life with what you were born with, and that which you acquire along the way, but it ain't the materials, it ain't the buying and the selling, but what you really acquire along the way. The truth is, the materials are anchors, and the electronics are noise. To get in touch with the Divine, you trip over the anchors, and the electronics cause too much interference.

What happens when you look at yourself in the world, alone in the Universe? What are you going to do? Do you have any choice? You're going to have to do the right thing…you have no choice. Without the materials or the electronics, you have to do the right thing, you have to help those that need it, and leave as clean a path as you can. It's very simple. My Karmic slate is clean. I have done what I have done because I had to, good or bad. I say more good than bad, but in the long run, you have to look out for each other, and just pick up the trash on your way

***

Chas Lee never talked too much about the man he killed. It was self-defense, but he never used the words "murder" or "killed". Like all of us in different situations, he did what he had to do. He wasn't proud of it, nor was he ashamed of it, it just happened, and it happened in the past. He told me the story once or twice, and I knew what happened, I knew what he meant. He was a killer the way we all are. It takes a while to deprogram when you have been instilled with all of the moral black and whites, but everyone knows, perhaps deep down inside, some more than others, how far you have to be pushed before you realize who you really are.

In today's civilized world, people put too much emphasis on the evil of killing. They have lost the Purity, the Holiness of killing, not "murder", not the predisposed, modern age interpretation of unprovoked, cold-blooded murder of an innocent, but the Purity and the Passion of the act. Killing is pure, and there is probably more inherent evil in theft than in killing. Theft is nothing more than a crime of greed and opportunity. Killing is an act that is siphoned from deep in the recesses of the heart. It is a Pure and emotional act, love and hate being two emotions that are exactly side by side in the overall scheme of things. Inherently, people are all killers. It has not been that long, "civilization" is merely the wallpaper on the house that God built. We are all animals out of control, usually under the false illusion that we do control our own destinies. It is arrogant for any of us to assume that we maintain any control over this vast and splendid Universe.

***

Ruby seemed like the perfect partner. I wasn't gonna waste my time with someone who wasn't gonna see things the same way I did. Me an' Ruby were gonna do good things, and with her background, I pitied her sadness, but with her view of how things should be, there wasn't a better pair that was gonna make the world a better place.

Ruby's charity came from her own need for help when it wasn't there for her. I pitied her sadness, but since I had seen her demons, since I felt her pain, there was no one better to understand and to help her. Ruby was gonna get better, and we were gonna do nothing but good deeds.

Ruby knew what had been done to her, she knew who had done it, and what it had done to her, what it done to her point of view. Ruby had a hard time with those demons. Ruby didn't have many friends, and when any of 'em hung around long enough, she'd either just up and leave, or dissect 'em enough to expose all their human imperfection before she moved on. There was no room in Ruby's life for those that weren't right, those that weren't pure. Little things would set her off, and the whole thing usually crashed right down on her. She used to ask me why all the shit landed right on her. I didn't think back then that she was looking for it, nor that she deserved it, but it was all in the way she reacted to it. Ruby just couldn't let things go, absolutely every injustice had to be dealt with, and Ruby was too pure to close her eyes to the evil around her. Once I asked her brother Mike, why she was so sensitive to negativity. Mike told me that Ruby was used to being a victim. Being a victim was what Ruby was best at, and if she and Mike would go someplace, if they'd go into a bar, Ruby would scan the joint, and use her powers to see who it was that couldn't be trusted, who not to sit near, and the like. I asked her about it once, and she said it was all because she was psychic. Psychic maybe, but I started to wonder why it was only the evil she could see.

***

Ruby said you had to rely on your instincts. In this impersonal and high-tech civilized world, it was all you had to go on, and instincts were what God gave you, so you had to listen to the inner voices. Me, I had a tough time all my life, being told I was too sensitive. Back in Connecticut, we weren't supposed to listen to the voices. Back in Connecticut, the teevee was supposed to block out the voices, and God was in the Bible, so there was no need to be listening to any voices anyway.

It was strange, I'd go to mandatory church every Sunday morning, and sit there, an outsider, wondering if everyone else was getting something out of it, getting in touch with the Divine. Were the angels swimming around the heads of every other one there, leaving me outside the door to Heaven without a proper translation?

Maybe they were all getting exactly the same thing out of it that I was. Maybe the simpler minds need less stimulation. Maybe suggestion was all they needed. I dunno, all I could compare it to was my first trip to the casinos of Atlantic City, watching all the gambling addicts, coma-like at the tables, disabled elderly in wheelchairs on oxygen, trying to run the whole bank of slots with no thought of tomorrow, but again, there I was, on the outside looking in. There I was back in church, sitting right there on the outside looking in, wondering if that was as close as I was gonna ever get to God.

***

Ruby had noticed that our paths had crossed, or were drawn near several times, and that it was obvious that fate had been working on getting us together for some time. Outside my kitchen window there on Ludlow Street, there faced another window through the airshaft where I used to talk to the lady who lived there, Betsy. It was like one of those "Honeymooners" kind of social things that often took place down there in the tenements of the Lower East Side. The buildings were that close and you were lucky to have a window and that neighbor right across from you was also lucky to have a window and as fate would have it, those windows were so close they almost connected. I never knew it, but at the time, Betsy was Ruby's best friend, and was steady for some time with Ruby's brother Mike. The number of times me an' Ruby were merely a few feet away from each other all those times she was visiting east from Tacoma was amazing. Well Ruby knew that there was a reason for all this, that fate had been getting us closer and closer, that fate ultimately led us to that New Year's Eve at the Cafe, when we finally met our destiny.

***

The funny thing about fate is that I used to think that *"this is the way it's supposed to be"* meant *"this is the way it's supposed to be forever."* At that point in my youthful mind, it hadn't occurred to me that my view of fate was merely an abbreviation of the way things were supposed to be, maybe for now, maybe for a while longer. "Forever" adds a whole surreal and ironically, finite definition to the concept of fate. *"That's the way it's supposed to be for now"* is the best you can hope for in this life. Coming from Connecticut, I had accepted a somewhat limited capacity for abstract thought, and had not yet ridded myself of the linear Leave It To Beaver point of view. I expected relationships to last and I expected that it was natural to find the "One," who would be the finale of my linear search, who would be my reward, the just desserts after which I would settle down and life's problems would melt away into ongoing domestic bliss.

Apparently I wasn't as far away from Connecticut as I had thought, as far away as I had hoped, but it also could have been the beginning of the end of the age where linear thinking and the dream of getting my just desserts had been a reality.

***

I guess I was always an outsider looking in, an observer on this plane, pure and simple. I never fit in, and after a short lifetime of looking at it, I realized it wasn't all the rest of them that were keeping me out, it was me. Something God put inside of me, something else that kept me outside, that made me a non-joiner. I never was a Boy Scout, never joined any clubs, didn't hang out with the guys, was not into sports, and I realized at a young age, that going to church was all a bunch of mind control. Controlled simple minds "sharing", all sharing what they thought the one next to 'em was experiencing, all pretending they felt it too, and maybe they all would get into Heaven by sharing secondary experience. It seemed like you couldn't get into Heaven alone, you had to get into Heaven in a group with glassy eyes. *"Let us all pray in Unison."*

Groups have always scared the hell outa me. Communal common thought, and all, be it the Army, the Baptists or the Hippies, communal common thought is what helped rise Hitler to power. For whatever reason, I could never see how with all this many people, with all this much life experience, with the infinite combination of possibilities, that you could assemble large groups of people that all professed to share the same thoughts, the same values, and I finally figured out that they were just too lazy and too scared to find out how deep they could go into their own thoughts, into their own reality. They were scared of the animal they would find within, scared of seeing something real that the church hadn't prepared 'em for, scared that they lacked the true moral backbone to confront the unknown, and still come out on top without doing the wrong thing. Truth is, groups keep people from hearing the voices, and from following their hearts. They got the Bible, they got the preacher, and they don't need the voices to confuse things now.

***

People used to ask me why I ended up with so many crazy women. I never looked for it, but it did seem to happen. To me no one was normal you got what you got. In New York no one's normal anyway, and there may be more action, more beauty and more bravery in insanity. It certainly ain't boring. "Normal" is just something that people create, something that people predict and look forward to, just to fulfill their own boring fantasy. Normal is something most people strive for, but it doesn't exist on this Earth. Here there ain't no normal. Normal is for Heaven. People can all die and go to Heaven and all be just like one another. In Heaven everyone can be perfect and normal, and nothing will happen and everyone will be blissful, but on this plane, on this Earth, something should happen, and when things happen, they aren't always predictable, they don't always follow the plan, they aren't always normal. "Normal" shouldn't and doesn't exist, not on this Earth, not here, not now anyway.

***

There is a certain insanity in staying sane. There exists a luxury in the ability to go off the edge without the fear of consequence. It always used to drive me nuts the way something would piss me off and eat away at me, and I'd start to feel the urges. I could feel the necessity toward going crazy, of moving closer to the edge. It's hard to tell if it was the Christian guilt and the subsequent fear of consequence, but there was something that always kept me painfully in control.

Acid was a tool that brought you closer to the Edge, and I think those that lost it, lost it from the total fear of seeing absolute stone cold reality right in front of their face. All the perfect corners and all the straight walls, and the damned teevee sets and such are supposed to keep everyone in their place. When the walls start to fade and melt away, and you finally kill your teevee, then it's time to watch out, 'cause then you got no more man-made sanity telling you how to act and react.

In a way I'm seeing that killers have more honor than thieves. Thieves take advantage of an opportunity for the purpose of greed. A killer however, is motivated from the heart, from the beyond, from pure passion, the ultimate purity, the ultimate act of Love. This is not true of the killers who kill in the commission of their crime of greed, but is true of those who disregard consequence, who step out of society's control and step into that instantaneous moment of Love that frees them from the sanity.

It's been close. There are times I know deep down in my heart, as we are all killers, that at that one moment of absolute pure Love, or in self-defense, the ultimate expression of self-love, we all would do it. It was part of Chas Lee's life, a life of artistic self-expression, of the kill-or-be-killed instantaneous, without-second-thought acceptance of the ultimate importance of your own life, your own life over one who holds no value on yours.

***

There's times, I can't quite put my finger on it, but there's times I think It's better to go over the edge. There's so many assholes on this Earth fucking things up, taking up space and putting nothing back. There's times I just sit tight, grit my teeth, maybe sometimes near the full Moon, ask my neighbor to hold my bullets for a few days, just in case, but I still don't know why there's so many stupid people on this Earth.

My departed Father used to say, *"This world is full of jerks and if you let 'em get you mad, then you're always gonna be mad."* It didn't make me feel any better at the time, back then when I had a lot of youthful anger. It comes back sometimes, and sometimes it doesn't. I guess back then I was pissed off a lot of the time, and these days it seems to only come up when someone does something right in my face. Sometimes I just wanna get rid of the assholes, but my neighbor you see, well she's got my bullets, and maybe for now I'll sit this one out.

***

It seems that Christianity and Leave It To Beaver have indeed softened humankind's reflexes into such a state of turn-the-other-cheek passivity, that we have truly lost our natural struggle to survive, and Christianity has indeed separated us from our animal ancestors. People now buy their industrial meat in sanitary poly-wrapped packages, but protest the act of hunting as "inhumane".

We are all on the brink. The world has already ended, but people are still attempting to make sense of it all. While prophets of doom await the Big Boom and survivalists stockpile for the aftershocks of nuclear annihilation, no one has slowed down enough to look at the basic, simple reality that exists right in front of us...the world has already ended. There were no explosions, no smoking craters, no nuclear mutants pillaging for the last remaining resources, but what is really happening? Mutants are crawling over the face of the Earth, foraging for the last precious resources, first minerals and precious metals and now water and clean air itself. Thievery is so high-tech and entrenched in this modern and "civilized" place we live in, it is part of the Corporate Culture, and is either unseen or just taken for granted. It has become commonplace, and the stigma of the crime won't ever be attached to the further plundering of our resources.

Human behavior in this civilized world, in this Modern Age, can only be likened to that of post-apocalyptic mutants roaming and plundering the Earth. We have returned to survival of the fittest, self-defensive existence while the turn-the-other-cheekers get up from the teevee to see if there's any more beer in the fridge. Reality has long since died. The world has ended and you've already missed it.

***

I guess "crazy" is a relative term, but I've got to admit I did attract some crazy women back in those days. Maybe it was me who brought out the crazy in them. Not too much bothered me back then, so they probably thought it was okay, and I wouldn't really mind anyway. Me, I always felt pretty normal, although I hate that word. "Normal" sounds like all those teevee arrogant families back there in the real world, but I saw myself as being "normal" like being without hang-ups or illusions. Even when I went off the deep end, I never saw it as a conflict I always came back.

I guess no matter how far off the deep end I went, I always saw the natural state, the sober mind, the mind devoid of drink, substances or illusions as the place to return to. There are people and there are places where there is no concept of the natural state. Maybe it changes. Maybe all the natural state is, is Survival. People do that which is necessary to survive, and therefore, "natural" is a better phrase than "normal".

My ideal girl, the way I saw it back then was a cheerleader on Acid. Back in high school, I was either too shy or they were too cool or a combination of the both, but cheerleaders were always way off limits, too much attitude, and too much effort. As things moved along, people started to get real or they stayed in Connecticut, but after some moving and experimenting and such, some very diverse paths would cross many miles down the road, many years later. The cheerleaders, those who had enough rebellion and individuality to experiment, not to live their parent's lives, some of 'em ended up being okay after all.

***

Some of 'em would even end up on Ludlow Street, standing in line, waiting. If they were pretty enough, their boyfriend would stand in line and wait for 'em, but they still ended up waiting, there's always some casualties. A little Acid, a little this, a little that, and moving on...the recipe to find out who you are, is never the same. See that cheerleader, years down the road, flying high and lovin' the handcuffs, that cheerleader has truly broken away, that cheerleader is ready to face the uncertainty of the future.

Breaking away doesn't have to be anti-social, just different-social. There's those that try to hang on to their own small reality, not really sure what it is. They're the ones that scare me the most. Their reality is the one that has to be everyone else's reality, because they see their mirror in others, they hang onto control, they don't have the security nor the peace of mind to accept what they see as the right thing, they have to force it on others. It's not that difficult, just take a deep breath, step forward, and see what happens, but they've got fear, so they've got the Boy Scouts, the Army, the fraternities, churches and such. There is strength in numbers, so they got to drag everyone in on it and never stray too far from the flock.

***

Now Ruby had a sense of justice. Having been done wrong herself, so long ago, so young and so helpless, Ruby kept her eyes open for the poor unfortunates. The trouble was, Ruby knew it was why she didn't keep a lot of friendships for very long. Ruby considered herself a mirror, and she knew that what people didn't like in her was what they didn't like in themselves.

I used to tell her that there was no curse on her, but she didn't believe me, she rarely believed me, she said that trust had to be earned. I had never wronged her, and I never lied to her, and I wasn't quite sure when that trust would finally be earned. I didn't think there was a curse on her, but at times she was the mirror and at times she was looking in the mirror. As time went on, Ruby had a hard time knowing if there was a difference between the two. There were times Ruby just wanted to take it easy, and fade on into the background like everyone else, but some new shit would always hit the fan and keep her on the same course. Something awful was always happening somewhere, and Ruby with her intuition just couldn't keep her eyes closed to it. It was always up to her to straighten things out. Ruby was the last honest person, the last savior of the helpless, so once it came her way, she had to help, she had to fight.

In her weak moments when Ruby had doubt, in those moments when Ruby confronted the curse that hung over her, I'd try to tell her how I saw it. I'd tell her that the bad things didn't come her way for any particular reason, but the problem laid in the way she reacted to 'em. I told her that this stuff was all over the place, and people couldn't feel everyone else's pain, and people couldn't fix all the bad things, not all the time anyway, but of course, Ruby didn't believe me, 'cause I hadn't earned her trust yet.

As much as I tried to tell her, and as much as I tried to show her that there was no curse on her, the more I knew, and the more I think she knew, that there was a dark curse that lingered deep inside of her, and it was fast becoming obvious to me, perhaps what she knew all along, that it wasn't going to go away.

***

Ruby's life hadn't been easy, but I never thought there was anything that couldn't be fixed. There's always a way to turn things around. Ruby had spent so much of her life struggling and trying to survive, that she never had any time to slow down, look around and enjoy what she did have. Lizzie was growing up, Ruby's family was on the other side of the world, and I was there, as fate put us together, for me to show her that life didn't have to be all that painful. I hadn't had a bad life, my family was so normal it seemed weird, but still I was alienated, I was still on the outside, and couldn't understand why people hurt each other so much, and I still held on to my youthful desire to be objective, and to see things the way they really were, not just the way I wanted to see 'em or the way I could have seen 'em through naïve Connecticut eyes, but seeing things as they really were, pure and untouched, like an outsider looking in.

Well I saw Ruby the way she really was, and I saw that all she needed was to have someone to look after her, to take care of her, so she'd see there were no demons, and that life was safe, and she could start enjoying life the way she should. We were put together because I was the calm in the eye of the storm, pure and focused in the wild torrent of insanity. I always landed on my feet, and was strong enough to stand beside her when times got tough. I would be the calm in the eye of Ruby's storm.

***

Things were getting rough on Ludlow Street. Shit was hitting the fan, and most of it seemed centered around Ruby. She hadn't been there long, but it didn't really take that much time. Ruby lived in one of Riley Fish's buildings and that in itself was a slap in the face. Riley Fish had bought three condemned tenements back when they had no doors and all kinds of junkies ran in and outa the place. I think those buildings cost around ten thousand dollars in those days. Any asshole with a checkbook could be a landlord in those days. Riley put doors on the buildings, but locks were too expensive, and for years Riley was takin' twenty dollars a week from whoever wanted to live there…Junkie Heaven, one week at a time. A funny thing happened sometime in the early eighties, and everyone from everywhere just had to live in New York City. If they were rich enough, they could almost live anywhere they wanted to, and most of us were Downtown, on the fringe. Edge living was okay, but some were just being outright ripped off, and seemed to love every minute of it. Riley Fish's place in life was to accommodate those masochists. People wanted to be ripped off by New York, and Riley Fish was glad to help.

Riley and his partner Joe Wolf took over those buildings, five story walkups, some with floors bowing deep into the downstairs ceiling with a toilet down the hall and a bathtub in the kitchen, those that had kitchens. Most were just one room "studios" maybe with a hotplate. Riley and Joe, with some money in the bank, finally put locks on the doors, carpet in the halls, a couple coats of cheap paint, and started paying off all the usual inspectors. For those capital improvements, Riley and Joe would get between $800-$1000 a month to, as the ad read... *"Live on a Safe, Sunny Block in the Quaint East Village"*. The sad thing was they always got tenants. There were always people ready to get beaten.

New York in those days was weird and gettin' weirder. There was a gravy train, and no one wanted to get off. From one end of Manhattan Island to the other, the rich were getting richer, the poor were getting high, and the passers-through just couldn't get enough. Just being in New York was all it took, but there were those that thought because some were getting rich, their own opportunities increased also. Me, I never paid more rent than I had to, but there were others who thrived on being ripped off. New York is full of adversity and there is always a thrill to the challenge of overcoming as much of it as you could. There comes a time though, when you wonder why this idiot keeps bragging about how many times he's been mugged, and what an asshole his landlord is.

***

Ruby rolled into New York for a change. She had been a mother to Lizzie her entire adult life, and wanted to move on for a while. Lizzie stayed with her father in Tacoma while Ruby went east to see what lay in store. Her brother had a small crib on the block, so Ruby looked for a place down on Ludlow Street. At $800 a month for a dingy pigeon hole, people were beginning to realize they could do better, which usually left ongoing vacancies in Riley Fish's buildings. Since it was convenient, especially in those days of a two-percent vacancy rate, Ruby checked right in to her overpriced, undersized pigeonhole and settled in.

Depending on how I felt about 'em, I'd either pity people who were at Riley and Joe's mercy, or just laugh. When I started getting to know Ruby, I had pity that someone I cared for so much was at the mercy of such a couple of greedy assholes. I took it personally that they were taking advantage of someone I cared for that much.

Months after we met, Ruby realized that she didn't want to stay in that same apartment anymore. Me, being a hopeless romantic, I was gonna help. Ruby didn't need Riley's shit, and at that point, I would have helped anyone break their lease with him. Riley never had a shortage of suckers waiting to give him money to live on a safe, sunny block in the quaint East Village, but Riley thought he ran the block. Riley was a real wanna-be, a mobster without a mob and the slightest question that he held status because he was the landlord of three, horrid shit holes down there on Junkie Street would have sent him off.

The day came, and Ruby and I were taking boxes and bags full of her stuff down the stairs, and across the street to Helen Fisk's store for storage. On the last trip down the stairs, the front door swung open, and in walked Riley Fish. I knew I was busted, but kept on going. I looked straight at him and straight past him and kept walking.

"Mornin' Riley," I mumbled.

"Taking a trip?" Riley came back at me, as I kept walking by.

"Taking a trip?" I thought to myself. Shit, burning this guy is easier than I thought it would have been.

"Yes, Riley, taking a trip." I squeezed past him, my arms full of Ruby's boxes.

I told Ruby it would be best if she laid low for a while. Riley was a chump, but it was best to avoid him and whatever drama he was gonna throw our way. A couple of weeks later, Ruby was holed up in my place across the street, and I bumped into one of Riley's flunkies who came charging at me from across the street. It seemed that me an' Ruby had stolen priceless antiques from the "furnished apartment" that Riley had rented to her, and they wanted them back. The thing was that most of those priceless antiques they described, and said were stolen, was actually furniture that Ruby brought with her from Tacoma. It was pretty obvious now that they had been in her place. They described her furniture in great detail. How many times, we weren't sure, and if she was there sleeping, we still don't know, but it sent a chill that they had been in her place maybe countless times. To make matters worse, they called the cops, and I was already spending more time than I wished keeping Ruby outa trouble.

***

Ruby was having trouble at work, and her job was having her followed because she had seen some sensitive documents she wasn't supposed to. She started to notice that everyone at work was beginning to avoid her. Her Human Resources Director told her they would recommend that she get a psychiatric evaluation, but Ruby said it was all part of her having seen those documents. As usual,

Ruby knew too much and there were those that would stop at nothing to stop her. At first, it didn't seem that any of this was her fault, but I started to see an ever-expanding web of trouble that seemed to grow all around her, and she attracted more and more trouble as time went on. Ruby was starting to lose it, and lamented about how hard it was to keep her head up, knowing that she was the only sane one, that she was the only one who was doing the right thing. She knew they were isolating her, identifying her as the crazy one, it was all part of their plan, just to keep her down, but Ruby was on to 'em and was not about to blink now.

***

Ruby was missing Texas, and me, I thought maybe we had both been in New York a bit too long. For me it was eight years, but everything was starting to wear thin. For Ruby, it was only about six months, but I could see it was already taking its toll. There was no reason for her to go through any more of this shit. New York was not for everyone, and I knew it was time for me to help her limit her losses and move on out.

Texas was slow and warm. Ruby was from a small town up north, and things were simpler there. Ruby remembered her childhood and would smile as the good times came back to her. It was as if the weight had somehow been lifted from her, and her entire being was lighter.

Ruby would remember the innocence of her school days, learning to ride a bicycle and taking long walks in the grassy fields of north Texas. She would remember the swing sets at the Town Park and the animals that lived at the Zoo. Ruby would become as calm as I had never seen her when her thoughts went back to Rigler, Texas.

It seemed that the best thing to do was to get her out of that hostile New York, show her there was no curse on her, and start living, living out a simple, more boring life. The money was in the bank, the Rent-a-Truck was sitting there with the motor running, there was no reason not to go, so up and go we did.

***

Shit had been hitting the fan, and I knew Ruby was never meant for New York, let alone the Lower East Side. I helped her bust her lease with Riley Fish, missing his $850 a month. Ruby holed up in my place, directly across the street, and for a couple of weeks, things were fine. I told Ruby these guys, Riley and his flunkies were spineless but never to underestimate 'em, and never to turn her back on 'em. Well Ruby, stubborn and steadfast, ended up so full of cabin fever, one day decided to up and take a walk down Ludlow Street and stretch her legs, and sure as shit before any time had passed, one of the vultures came swooping down, and me up in my pad heard the screaming down there in the street. Brass knuckles on one hand and a chain wrapped around the other, I ran down there as fast as I could, and there he was, maybe an unwitting accomplice, but an accomplice of Riley nonetheless, had cornered Ruby in Helen Fisk's store. Helen lived across the street from Riley, she knew him well, and knew there was no doubt what was going on. She knew Riley and she knew not to trust him. Helen locked Ruby inside, and left this asshole banging on her door like it was the end of the world. By the time I came down, Riley Fish had joined his henchman, and I swept in with a vengeance.

Shortly afterward, Henchman was on the sidewalk, trying to pick himself up from all fours, either looking for a contact lens or his teeth, or whatever, while Riley Fish was trying to keep from shitting in his pants, not ever having had anyone call his bluff like that. Meanwhile, Ruby had called the cops from inside the store and ironically had charges filed against Riley, Joe and Henchman, with no mention of the missing teeth. Interestingly, Riley developed an apprehensive respect, both for me, Ruby, and for his still-intact teeth, and became my best friend in the world after that incident. *If you can't beat the shit out of 'em, join 'em.*

***

Now people are like animals, or more precisely, people are animals, outa control, following Biology, following nature, following the DNA. Only technology evolves. If you look at it, human behavior, which is the same as animal behavior, has never changed. The weapons have gotten highly evolved, and we have cars that drive us home to our new teevees, which in turn tell us what to do, and which newer technological items to buy, but people as a rule are still ignorant, stupid motherfuckers, blindly following instinct, maybe even modern instinct, but following whatever, nonetheless. Those that do seem to rise above, maybe through Divine inspiration, get the notion to step just a little bit aside or above, perhaps not evolving at all, but at least observing the whole fucking mess from a different perspective.

Now I've never been an intimidating sort, never been overly aggressive, but for some reason, I have always been seen to others as some kind of a challenge. Being like that usually put me right in the center of the animal male behavior. For some reason, I quite often found myself being confronted by some macho wanna-be asshole trying to challenge me, always in some physical, aggressive posture. In different places and at different times, there'd be these chinless intellectuals, highly evolved in some sort of self-perceived, over educated manner, attempting to convey the same animal behavior on an intellectual level, thinking they were high above the dog pack, but still bein' that same dog trying to piss on your tree.

Me, I learned the hard way. The Puritans taught me to *"turn the other cheek"*. It defies the survival instincts that have brought the animals to the present state. Man, who feels that he is above the animals has a self-important, Holier-than-thou newly acquired instinct. We don't need to fight, we are better than defending ourselves, so we turn the other cheek. To me it seems like a one-way ticket to extinction.

It's a slow climb uphill, regaining your lost instinct. If you went to Harlem and told everyone to quit eating that slave food, you'd probably get shot. How do you reclaim that which has been lost? How far back do you have to go to get real? Where did one thing stop and the other begin? Somehow over the years, I couldn't ignore the voices. It came back to me like it never left. Survival, integrity, self-reliance and self-defense were traits long lost in the hygienic sanity of the Connecticut suburbs. Slowly over the years I learned to search for all that had been lost.

The dog who's been put in his place, instead of going in the corner to lick his wounds, all of a sudden wants to be your best friend in the whole world. The weak who thought they were strong will follow the top dog until the next defeat.

***

Things were starting to get weird and I couldn't quite put my finger on it. Ruby did not have a happy life, but I figured that since we were together now, all she needed was to see that things could be okay. I'm not quite sure when she told me that I was the first man that she ever loved, but it made perfect sense to me. She had been married once, and I never kidded myself that she didn't tell him, I just figured that was how she felt in her mind at that time, and that was okay. I never needed accuracy, just sincerity.

There were a few weird things, Ludlow was a very small block with a lot of action going on, and it was inevitable that my past would come our way. Ruby could not forgive that I had a past. Ex girlfriends, ex ships in the night, deals and more deals, all gone to the winds of the past, but Ruby expected a thirty three year old virgin with no past, a man with no ghosts. I asked her if she honestly expected to meet a grown man with no past, but as usual, Ruby did not see things the way I saw them. To me, life was an "either or" equation...you were either with it or you were off of it, but to Ruby nothing was ever quite right. For whatever reason, she couldn't accept the logical progression that my past had led me to where I was at that time and place. Hell, without that past, there would have been something wrong. Life is for tasting and taste I did. Ruby hated the fact that I even had a past. Ruby had Nigel, her ex-husband, and they had their daughter Lizzie. Ruby had an estranged family, and God knows whatever else she had done, but none of that mattered, it was my past, the fact that I even had a past at all, that was gonna forbid us from having our own happy life together. In my blind Connecticut fashion, I assumed she'd grow out of it.

I decided that I was gonna be the perfect mate to Ruby. I'd been there, done that for so long, it was time to focus everything into this, this new adventure. I pursued that relationship with the same level of intensity and involvement as anything that was put in front of me at that time.

I used to cook at a restaurant there in Rigler with Joe Small, boy wonder. Joe had always been the prodigy of Rigler and was almost graduated from high school, one semester away from starting at Texas A & M. Joe could burn water, Joe was thoroughly useless in a kitchen, but like so many other Texans I had yet to meet, he was someone's relative, so Joe worked in the kitchen. I tried in vain to show him how to do things, but Joe had better things on his mind, Joe was on his way to the Aggie stronghold and none of this other common shit really mattered to him. Joe was going to college soon and Joe was on his way. One night, and another tray of burnt enchiladas later, I finally pulled him aside and asked him what would happen if he got hit by a car tomorrow. He drew back, confused.

"Joe," I said, "if you died tomorrow, God forbid…do you wanna be remembered as the guy who almost went to A & M, or do wanna be remembered as the guy who did the best he could at what was in front of him at that time? You really seem disinterested in what is right here, right now. You seem to have everything wrapped up in something that hasn't even happened yet…"

Joe, in all his infantile wisdom, the boy wonder of Riger, Texas, with all his lofty aspirations, had never had to confront that which was right in front of him. Joe who usually had something aloof and typically condescending to say, remained quiet and left work that night, silent and somewhat confused.

***

I pretty much didn't get high anymore, I didn't go out unless Ruby wanted to go for a drink together. I left the string of nameless faces behind for a quiet, safer and more predictable life, but Ruby said my past had already proved to her that I was unfaithful.

***

Ruby used to say that trust had to be earned, that no one was innocent, and over time the trust would have been earned. Blissful in my ignorance, I set out to settle down and help Ruby have a secure life. I stayed home at night, helped around the house, and regrettably had to send my collection of girlfriend photos to my brother back in Connecticut. I told Ruby, quite truthfully, that I had gotten rid of them. The more I showed Ruby the trust she could have in me, the more she knew there was something below the surface that she had to keep a vigilant eye on. Ruby was not about to be fooled by my deceit.

One night, back there in New York, ignorant in my newly found marital bliss, I was cleaning the shack, vacuuming, cleaning things up, when out of the blue Ruby kicks in, rage in her eyes, accusing me of *thinking* about other women. She knew because I liked sex, and because I liked a lotta sex, that it was on my mind, and it was on my mind with other women. It wasn't her I wanted, and she knew that there in her living room, doing all that housework, that I was cheating on her with other women. Ruby was no fool, she knew what was on my mind, and was not about to be taken for a fool while she drank hot tea at the kitchen table.

Ruby became a lunatic, running through the apartment, screaming and throwing things. She had caught me cheating pure and simple, and she was not gonna put up with it. I responded in a manner that cut Ruby deep in the heart. I committed the unforgivable sin, one that probably led to our ultimate demise. I took a deep breath and told her I wasn't gonna fight with her, that I didn't like seeing her all out of her head like she was, and she could stay home and do what she needed to do, but I didn't have time for this.

"Ruby, this seems like this is something you feel you have to do. I'm going out for a while. When you're done fighting, don't forget to turn out the lights!"

I went out alone to take a walk. Ruby was looking for a fight, about what I'm not sure, I was never sure, but I wouldn't give it to her. We were married, and I swore to look out for her best interest. I don't know what you're supposed to give a loved one, but that night I decided that I wasn't gonna give her what she thought she wanted, but I was gonna give her what I felt she really needed.

That night I took a long walk down by the river, quiet with a forty of something cheap in a paper bag, then a long walk through no man's land, to test the waters. I was pissed off, so pissed off, even the muggers avoided me. I could smell their fear. The hunter can become the hunted in a split second and I enjoyed the harmony of reversing the order of things, if only for a little while. Hours and a coupla forties later, I stumbled back home. I came back hours later, knowing it would have given her time to cool off, calm down, and go to sleep. I didn't wanna deal with any more of her bullshit, I didn't want her to provoke another fight, so I took my sweet time, but when I got back, all the lights were on, and Ruby was frantically packing her bags.

There she was, furiously packing as if her life depended on it. The irony was that I had left several hours earlier and there she was still packing. Timing was the essence of Ruby's drama. We had been married only about a month at this point, but oh, was she pissed off, and yes Ruby was leaving. Ruby had every right to be mad, married only a month and her man was already cheating on her, thinking about other women while he vacuumed the living room rug. There it was, one-thirty in the morning, and there was Ruby packing her bags in a hurricane of intense fury. I had no idea I was gonna come home to find her still awake and in this advanced state of psychosis, and I realized that it would be best if I tried to calm her down. I wanted to help her. I never liked to see her hurt, so I calmly asked her, *"Baby...where you gonna go?"* There was a silence so sudden and so thick you could cut it with a knife. She stopped and looked over at me confused, and in another second went right back to dramatically packing her bags, arms flailing. She ranted about how she never shoulda married me, but that it was over now, and she was finally leaving so Fuck me.

I asked her again, *"so where is it you're gonna go? It's one-thirty in the morning in New York City, baby and we don't have a car, where are you gonna go?"* She hated the control that my calm and rational demeanor had over her ongoing drama.

"I hate you, you asshole!"

"Yeah, I know Ruby, now unpack your bags and come to bed, okay?"

She tried to get me to fight with her when there wasn't really anything to fight about. Even if I won, which was never easy, I would have lost since it was always her fight and her drama I was being drawn into. Perhaps a sign that I didn't really love her, I chose to stay on the outside of her drama, I refused to get involved in Ruby's own battle with herself.

To this day I don't know what love is, but I don't think that embellishing it with drama does any good. Life is spontaneous and dramatic enough, but home life should be the sanctuary, the calm from the storm. Ruby didn't really understand sanctuary. Ruby just didn't see it the same way I saw it.

***

Ruby started working in midtown for an HMO provider in the Sales office. She found herself surrounded with fresh-outa-college wanna-be Yuppies in new suits they bought with their first Visa card. They'd show up on Monday morning, bragging about their big hangover and that great lesbian photo shoot in the latest Penthouse magazine. *"Boy would I do some things with those two!"* they proudly boasted. In their own mind, they were heroes. Ruby had a hard enough time with men, but this new job was about all she could take. One day she walked in to find her boss, grinning like a naughty twelve-year old, as he ran "blowjob" through the spell-checker on his desktop computer.

Ruby was having a tough time hanging on, and I can't say I blame her. Me, I had been in a locker room before and I could speak the language. I didn't really like to speak the language, but it's best to know how to communicate on all levels. It's funny really, you can know and understand all the same stuff, but it's how you live your life. The ones that get the least, talk about it the most. I was ten or eleven when I was first told how babies were made. Dad wanted to make sure I knew, because his father before him never told him, and Dad's learning curve came from lessons learned in the locker room, on the street corner, and later in the Army. It was sometime, a few years later when the locker room jocks first found out about sex, and they were outa their heads over it. Young boys giggled at the lamest jokes as they were tossed around on the school bus every day. Even back then, through twelve-year-old eyes and ears, I knew from bullshit, and here I was twenty years later, facing the same assholes with the same limited awareness and over-inflated self-image. Penis-wielding bravado had always been boring and redundant, but no one had told them, so they bragged on. By that point, I could have sent my own photos, my own stories…endless volumes, into Penthouse magazine and kept on sending 'em, but there they were, the spectators, inadequate on the sidelines, wishing they could get into the big show. It's amazing how the Corporate world doesn't weed out the weak and pathetic from its ranks, and it's increasingly obvious that the impotent and insecure, wearing their new power tie, are taken in, and are protecting each other, and are running Corporate America.

Ruby was irate, and couldn't even feign transparent support for the inadequate whitemen at work. She came home every day, increasingly pissed off, to the point where it was painful for her to go in to work in the morning. Finally, aware that she was trouble, the locker room found a reason to terminate Ruby. All of a sudden when the shit hit the fan, the wall went up and it became *"us against them"… "us against her…"* Ruby started coming in to a wall of silence every day. Her best friend Lucia stopped talking to her at the same time she was given a promotion and a cash bonus. The Human Resources Director told Ruby that she would be sent for a psychological evaluation, due to her alienation and her obvious lack of a "team-player" attitude. Me, I could have puked.

***

The trouble was that Ruby's fears all had a foothold in reality. I don' think any of her situations started from nothing, but Ruby, Ruby could never let anything go, she always fed it, and she always let it grow and grow into the next adversary she had to conquer.

Ruby lived for the drama and her life was never boring. After the work incident, them pushing her out, having her followed and all, Ruby just couldn't let go. Ruby knew they were coming into our house at night, trying to find out what she really knew, looking for documents, having her followed everywhere she went. Ruby at that time, had been considering filing a lawsuit for harassment, and she knew that they were after her. The lawsuit was the only way the locker room would be infiltrated. The men's club needed to be taken down and Ruby knew that she was the one to do it.

I loved Ruby's drama, but she was getting way over her head at this point. She wasn't sleeping at night, and every New York City noise reminded her that they were out there, watching her and waiting. I had to step back, back from Ruby's newly found demons, and separate myself from her fearful life, and think. I loved her drama, but it was time to step back and figure out what to do next. Ruby was about ready to combust, and I had never seen anyone that close who hadn't fully lost it. She was close and getting closer all the time. I couldn't see how she still hung on. I tried to stay detached, but insanity is contagious. It was very hard to sleep at night, that close to her demons. I could hear them inside her, I could feel them breathe. It was time to step back and look at my own sanity. It was time to step outside and look in, for the good of both of us.

Ruby was missing Texas, and me, I thought maybe we both had been in New York just a little too long. For me it was eight years, but it was all starting to wear thin. For Ruby it had been only six months, but I could already see it taking its toll. There was no reason for her to go through any more shit. Texas was warm and things were slow there, things would be simpler in Texas. Ruby had this feeling that if she went back, things'd be like they were when she was young, and maybe if she didn't have that chance to start over again, that maybe Lizzie could start out and have the life, the happiness and the innocence of youth that Ruby had missed out on. I felt that the best thing to do was to move on with her, to help her settle down in Texas, and show her that there was no curse on her, that it was all New York and the adversity that comes with it. It wouldn't be that hard to leave her demons behind her and to start living a simple life. Me, I was ready for a more boring life, I'd had enough stimulation for a while, and they hadn't killed me yet. Still standing and still breathing was always a good day. Money was in the bank, the truck was waiting so on a cold autumn day, we up and left New York. Ruby was leaving again, but this time I was leaving with her.

TEXAS, INTERMISSION, OR WHATEVER...

I don't know…I didn't really get married expecting to get laid a lot. I don't think I got married for the excitement of it. I guess I got married for consistency. There was a lot of sex before marriage, and there was a lot of strange sex before marriage. You never knew how the night would end or with whom. There was a long procession of strange women, some of whom defied convention, some of whom were outright bizarre. I tried to leave the dangerous ones behind. It was exciting, but as time went on, it became the same, it became the same faceless woman, it became boring and repetitious. Life between those amorous encounters was outright lonely and afterglow only lasted so long.

Many a night after everyone had left, I would sit, or sometimes lie on the floor on my back alone, teeth grinding, examining all those faces in the cracks in the ancient plaster of my ceiling. It was cold and lonely, and I'd think there had to be a better way. Sex is a lot like drugs, you get your thrills, but it can only last so long, and if you minimize the damage, getting out intact is a reasonable goal.

It's funny, marriage is a lot like Acid…to each person who partakes of it, there is a separate and different reaction. To me, marriage would be an extension of the way things were, only on into perpetuity, although I never really looked that far down the road. I was ready for something different and I guess Ruby was as different as it could get. I couldn't really go any further into the other direction, I had already gone down that road as far as I cared to and I guess I was ready for some new Acid, and Ruby was new Acid, untested and unproved as yet, but new Acid nonetheless.

***

Ruby's past had a lot of blanks in it, and there was a definite lack of continuity in her recollections of it. I guess at that time, that didn't bother me too much, because at that time I was cleansing all traces of linear existence out of my reality. I was stripping myself of the Connecticut linear reality that had for so long dominated the way things were with me.

I hadn't really thought that the blanks were that dubious, as Ruby's life had obviously been filled with a lot of pain and a lot that was best left alone. Ruby knew all about the demons and when they came in, she knew all about the cause and the effect. To me the blanks were more survival than denial. There was no sense dragging up old issues, the past was the past, and we were all adults, we were all out on our own. The reality of life is painful enough without the admission of any more reality and any more pain than the brain can handle. I knew Ruby would fill the blanks when the time was right.

***

I had been with a lot of scared women and I had been with a lot of scary women, nothing back then really seemed to phase me. Back then it was all Punk Rock; there was Mindy, back there in Connecticut with all those scars on her wrists, and Zelda in New York, with her scars invisible, but much deeper nonetheless. I never really thought that the normal were to be avoided, but they did tend to be boring. Normal lives never held much interest to me. Me, I came from a normal Leave It To Beaver Connecticut family, with its linear realities, and I had to stop the cycle somewhere...I knew that too much normal was bound to curse this Earth.

When Punk Rock first kicked in back then, Connecticut was the best place to be. It wasn't all that wild, but when the Punks started trying on the choke chains and dog collars in the pet aisle at the local Five and Dime, the Puritans all ran to church, praying that this wasn't the Armageddon. It was wild and it was different and normal bored me. I guess I directed my own path and in the process, ended up in the company I deserved.

I looked down at Mindy, all fours tied to the corners of the bed, blindfolded with her taut stomach glistening from the whiskey. The opium made time lunge forward and surge back. I looked down at her scars, glad she hadn't finished the job. She was warm and wet, a wild animal breathing hard, pulsating there in front of me on the sheets of that questionable bed in that cheap motel on the Berlin Turnpike outside of Hartford. "Rates by the Hour" as the sign read. It was Karmic surreality in Connecticut, and it sure beat grazing with the flock of sheep.

***

Suzie Lo wanted me to beat the shit out of her. Suzie Lo was a strange one, an Art Director for a midtown ad agency, fulla Martini lunches and Happy Hour before going back to her 14 hour work day, back to the office and an ounce of coke at home to make sure she didn't miss anything. Suzy Lo had a tortured life, her father was Jewish and Chinese, neither culture would ever accept the other. Suzie Lo's father owned buildings all over town, and Suzie would someday have as much money as the old man was ever gonna have. Suzie Lo was never gonna be happy. Suzie lived with some NYU professor, but she liked my youth and stamina. One night Suzie took me to one of her co-ops, empty and dark, large and soaring, laid her fur coat on the hardwood floor and slowly undressed in front of me, beckoning me to join her. I was out of it from all the blow she had fed me, I could have cared less about much of anything at that point.

Suzie wanted us to kill an eight-ball as quickly as possible as soon as we got to the loft. Rails on the mirror disappeared more quickly than I thought possible. The first blast hit the back of my head and that was all-she-wrote! My heart raced and my head soared. I only helped her with the rest of it to be polite. I wasn't sure what her hurry was but I kept up the pace. My eyes were watering and I couldn't feel my face. Hell, I couldn't feel my body. Suzie beckoned me but sensed my disinterest. I was really snowed under, and Suzie was getting irate. All she had to do was participate but I had to regroup and focus, I had to perform and please her, for how long? Time stood still as I watched the dull glow of distant lights peek out between the dark shadows that danced on the walls. Suzie Lo poisoned me and then wanted me spry and healthy. She shook her head and with a crazed look in her eyes, she suddenly punched me in the chest.

"I want you to hit me. HIT ME YOU ASSHOLE!"

I realized that if the party was gonna go on, and if I wasn't gonna fuck her then I would have to beat her. I stopped and tried to focus for a minute. The shadows continued to roll down the walls around us as the dull lights flickered in the corners of my eyes. She got madder and louder...

"HIT ME YOU FUCKER, I DON'T LIKE YOU ANYWAY!"

I knew she wasn't talking about pinching or slapping. Suzie was not gonna be satisfied until I beat the holy living shit outa her...she wanted it then and there, and she wanted it hard. Fucking or fighting...

I pictured her bloody in the hospital then I flashed to her professor boyfriend, chinless intellectual, weak and ineffective, but hiding in the closet nonetheless, with a pistol making him top dog, making him strong. I saw me with a bullet in my head. Whatever it was, whatever it was she really wanted, I saw this as just a step on the other side of complete and total weirdness, and she could walk through Central Park at that early hour in the dark morning if she really needed to be bloodied that bad, but I still felt that her putting me in that chair was irresponsible and inconsiderate. I knew she wanted to be fucked and how badly she wanted to be fucked over, and I could see how much she wanted it. I decided to rough her up so badly she'd never forget it. I decided to give her the beating she so badly desired.

A true sadist in the company of a true masochist seemed like the perfect match. *What to do, what to do?* I slowly reached over and started putting my socks on. I took a deep breath and reached for my pants. As I got dressed, I stood up and looked down at her, naked…her breasts heaving under the force of her heavy breathing, her mussed-up jet black hair, with a distant rage in her eyes, saliva running off her chin. I looked down at her, and without much thought, I said…

"You know Suzie, I've done some weird things in my day, but this shit is baby food! Goodnight!"

I turned and walked out the door of her overpriced Theater District coop.

***

There was a cold chill in the Four-in-the-morning air as I made my way slowly down the eight blocks south to 42nd Street. My heart still raced and my teeth clenched as my mind kept reeling, and I looked at the junkies and the whores with nowhere to go and I wasn't sure myself where I wanted to go. I leaned on the corner, the northeast corner of Eighth Avenue and 42nd Street, hovering over the stairwell that descended down to the "A" Train that took forever to come, amid the clutter and confusion, and then the Clarity hit. For a brief moment in time, I looked around and I realized that there was no difference between me and them. There were no lines, there were no boundaries...I was they and they were me, and we were all lost.

Suzie called my machine three times a day for the next few days, sometimes weeping, trying to say something to correct all the insanity. Suzie kept grasping, Suzie whom I had only know for a couple of weeks, attempting to reach out and fix things that were deeply embedded, that were far beyond repair. Suzie called for days, to the machine, then finally gave up. Deep down I guess I gave her what she really wanted. I hope the pain was enough. Good-bye Suzie Lo.

***

Towards the end of our thing in New York, Ruby kept talking about Texas. Her father, being in the military an' all, had moved 'em around every year of her life, and Texas was the only home she ever knew. She was born up in north Texas, in Rigler near the Red River, just south of Oklahoma. She ended up back there and graduated from high school, and had lived elsewhere in Texas off and on. As time went on, Ruby realized that her only home was back there in Rigler. Ruby didn't want Lizzie going to any New

York City school, Ruby didn't want Lizzie going anywhere but Rigler High.

The more New York got on Ruby's mind, the more she talked about Rigler like a long lost friend. Me, I was a little leery of all the romanticizing, but I was tired of New York too. I was tired of the noise and the junkies. I was tired of constantly watching my back, and was getting just a bit old too be dodging the cops, spray can in hand. All in all it seemed like a good time to get out while the gettin' was good.

I've always liked Texas and usually had liked the Texans that I met. Usually they were friendly and a lot less provincial than some of those New York intellectuals would want you to believe. In New York they said to me, *"waddaya gonna do in Texas, join the Klan?"* In Texas they said, *"Wow, New York City, what's it like up there?"* Some of those smug New Yorkers seemed to be more narrow-minded than the rural Texans they judged so harshly.

New York is a big small town. The whole world passes through there at one point or another, and consequently New Yorkers will tell you all about "The Europeans" this, or "The Japanese" that, even though they only met the tourists passing through from those places, but most of those enlightened urbanites wouldn't ever sink so low as to cross the river to go to a party in Brooklyn, staying on their eighteen mile stretch of concrete at the peak of technological evolution.

***

Only technology evolves. People…see people are all still animals, living in caves, acting out of fear, and the behavior in however many years of evolution, has never advanced, but technology...technology is what is evolving...the weapons have all advanced, but the raw animal instinct that craves those weapons has never changed since the Dawn of Time. People, now in the midst of this technological evolution are convinced that since the technology and the weapons and such, have advanced by their own hands, that these, the makers of these weapons, of this technology, have highly evolved from the animal state. Well, it's the weapons and the weapons only that have evolved and maybe from the Beyond, those weapons have summoned the mere animals to this creation, but people, people, humans, whatever... have never evolved. People are still frightened animals living in caves. Technology has evolved. A semi-automatic is far superior to a revolver anyway.

***

So all that's evolved is my concealment .380, and at the pinnacle of Creation, it could evolve into an AK-47, and those higher-evolved weapons got the politicians in servitude, ready to blow up the world, which isn't really my concern, but I'm an animal with a somewhat evolved piece of weaponry that has chosen to own me, to own me in my fear, living in my cave, cowering and trying daily to please the God that controls me, but my .380 gives me less fear, and for that I am grateful.

I don't know why people try to settle their differences. Problem resolution is merely a fantasy of Western Civilization, brought to fruition by the teevee age, but maybe that's what we all want anyway since we all flock to the teevee with such blind obedience.

Me, down the road I got rid of my teevee and VCR and I got my .380 and my 9 millimeter semi-automatic. I guess that says something of the evolution of problem resolution. Hell, there ain't problem resolution.

***

Ruby, I can't say exactly what Ruby thought. In one light, she'd decry human behavior, excuse me, "male behavior" as if there was a specific thing that was keeping humankind from being what it should be. Ruby however, did not see cause-and-effect relationships. Ruby did not see that everything was part of a greater whole, and Ruby most of all, could not see, would not see, that if this one thing didn't happen, then the next thing in progression wouldn't happen. No, Ruby saw everything that was bad, and only if she were in control of things, then things'd be better, but for all her pissing and moaning, she didn't ever really have a solution, just a view of the things that shouldn't be the way they were. Ruby was caught in the web of an imperfect world, but if only everyone would just let her make the decisions, then the right decisions would be made...

So everything would be better in Texas, me and Ruby could start over, even though we'd barely started at all at that point. Ruby thought I'd leave all my trophies back in New York, so she could forget I ever had other women, and she could be home again, and Lizzie, Lizzie could have the life Ruby should have had, but never had the chance.

So there we were, driving south and west in the Rent-a-Truck, with my car in tow, with Ruby in the lead in her wagon like we were the pioneers heading west in the modern wagon train.

***

Ruby just couldn't figure out male behavior, she'd never admit it though. To Ruby, no one understood male behavior better than she did. Ruby knew exactly what was wrong with the world and who was fucking it up. The sad thing was that Ruby was an unwavering heterosexual, never had any inclination toward making love with women, but Ruby also didn't really have much use for men. Except for sex. Now here was one of Ruby's big dilemmas...men were obsessed with sex, men who only knew how to follow their dicks around for life, was why the world was such a fucked-up place. Children were abused and women debauched, so men with their blind sex drive was the reason civilization was crumbling. Ruby's problem was she too, shared that same sex drive, she loved that dick as much as the next woman and deeply hated herself for loving that dick. Ruby could live her life without men, had no use for 'em. Ruby would pontificate about how much she didn't need men, could care less whether they existed or not, and knew that the world would be a better place without 'em, but every once in a while Ruby had that itch that only a man could scratch.

Again, Ruby couldn't see the obvious "either/or" irony of life. In this case, *"either men exist at all, or there would be none at all"*...not even the good ones, but no, Ruby just didn't want men to exist at all, except me, and maybe her favorite uncle, Uncle Lem Grady down there in Rigler, but the rest of 'em could just crawl up and die. Once in a while she even expressed concern and affection for her father, who through it all, really loved and cared for her and in the next breath, she wished he'd die a slow painful death...out loud, for the whole world to hear, taunting the ever-present Karma, toward the ever increasing spiral of her own misery.

There were times Ruby would talk about how fucked up my family was, and even though everyone was relatively happy, Ruby knew that was only on the surface, and we were really miserable deep down inside, and even though her family stayed in touch and really had little or nothing to say to one another, they were the ones that had the true love a family should have for one another. Ruby would go on about how her father was a true man who really loved his family the way a father should, and that was the way a father should be, to the point that Ruby would soon remember how her father really was, how he was when she was young, what really happened, and she'd wish him dead again.

***

Ruby had the political climate behind her at that time. Reports of child abuse were selling newspapers and magazines like crazy, and all men were suspect. Hell, being a white male gave me the choice of any of the guilt I could stand. Whatever was fucked up was a man's fault and if it was real fucked up, it was sure to have been a white man behind it. Men were responsible for the molestation of women and children, and no one was safe. My Karmic slate was clean, but every night on the news and every day on the talk shows, Ruby would sit, glued to the teevee, reinforcing that men were all a bunch of fucked up assholes who'd fuck anything that couldn't fight back. Ruby knew more day after day, what a bunch of fucked up cowards we all were. Except me...sometimes, and Uncle Lem, and sometimes her father, but not usually.

Ruby's brother Mike was a flagrant and flaming homosexual. Well, at least that's the way Ruby knew things really were. Mike exhibited no such tendencies, usually was in the company of his girlfriends, and such, but did also have a circle of male friends. Now Ruby, with no friends to speak of, still couldn't comprehend male behavior. Though no harm had been done, Ruby was convinced that all these men congregating together all the time, well there was something there that just wasn't right, people shouldn't be that close. Now I feel that it probably all runs back to our animal lineage, but dogs do run in packs, all following after the senior, dominant dog. Since the female of the species keeps the nest, she is not usually as socially outgoing as the males is, but males run in packs, following the alpha dog and piss wherever it is they see fit. Regardless of the reason, there is the basic tenet of human behavior, and Mike's group was a microcosm of all that was wrong with the male of the species. No, they weren't molesters, but with all that peer support, Ruby knew it was only a matter of time before they ended up followied their evil inclination toward power and control, and meanwhile they were all just a bunch of horny gay men.

***

I'd have to say that before I met Ruby, I would have called myself a feminist. My inclination was toward compassion for and comradery with the female of the species more so than with the males and their pissing behavior. There was a time when I was younger, obviously naive and somewhat foolish, when I thought that the two sexes could be equal, and other than the obvious physical differences, people were just people. The truth was, it didn't take me long to realize the error of that theory and the differences were endless. Nonetheless, I've always liked women, truly liked women and I have loved women. Ruby used to tell me she knew I was the one for her because I genuinely liked women. I never had a sister, and over the years, women were always a mysterious force to be pondered and understood. By the time I first discovered sex, I became totally enamored by the uniqueness of the female. They were soft and precious, caring and unique. Sex was always a motivating factor, but it wasn't always necessary. I would usually cringe with embarrassment at the behavior of a typical horny male, shamelessly chasing his dick throughout life, self-respect be damned.

I went to the gym, chewed tobacco, spat and talked dirty. I'd smoke some, chew Blotters with the guys on a Friday night, and it was not uncommon in those days to bring handcuffs along on a casual date. In the long run, however, I felt my maleness was unique, and I tired quickly of the old, boring locker room humor, and what appeared to be either fear, confusion, or a genuine hatred of women. I used to see the total irony of the steroid-ridden macho jock whose penis-wielding bravado was so obviously a wall, a wall because his high school sweetie had dumped him some ten years prior. Get over it Bubba.

***

So Ruby saw in me a purity, a life devoid of abuse or obsession with sexual excesses. Perhaps it was my lingering Connecticut naiveté that she later detested so, but nonetheless, in those early days, she saw my genuine interest and affection for the female of this species, and in its purity, and she found refuge. For a while.

***

The wagon train to Texas could have been a vacation, but wasn't. Ruby and me had a three-day honeymoon back in New England, and then back to New York it was. In years prior, in single male sanity, in those pre-Ruby years, I'd just up and go. If I ever needed a vacation, work wasn't that important, so with future and career on hold, who cares if it's going on my permanent record, I'd just up and go whenever the ocean called, or the desert, or the mountains. People need time off, but Ruby was on a nonstop roller coaster ride, hanging on tight so she wouldn't fall off, and there was no place or time for relaxing. While she bemoaned the lack of a calm center in her life, there would be no relaxing in Ruby's world. I was only beginning to see that part of her.

So on the way down to Texas, I thought it'd be nice to stop in Nashville for a few hours...I'd only ever driven by, and hadn't ever had the chance to slow down and see the town, but Ruby wouldn't hear of it. Ruby wasn't gonna be happy 'til we got her safely back to Rigler. Rigler was her only home, even though in her entire life, she spent only a total of three years there. Rigler, Texas was the only safe place for Ruby. Strange enough though, her past was riddled with inconsistencies and contradictions, and as close as I could figure, Rigler was where her Daddy had had his way with her. As time went on, I began to question Ruby's reality. I was starting to become concerned that with all the inconsistencies and contradictions, there may only be room for Ruby in Ruby's reality.

***

On the wagon train ride south, the Sun was getting warmer and the breeze just cut right through me. The Sun smiled at me, so I pulled the truck over, somewhere on the rolling plains of northeast Texas and I got out and just started loving that Texas air. I closed my eyes and I breathed in slowly and deeply. Since Ruby was in the lead, she must have noticed me pulled over in her rearview mirror.

She stopped up ahead and whipped her car around and got out, looking at me kind of funny, and asked me…

"What are you doing? What's wrong? Why did you stop the car?"

I smiled calmly and told her that I was breathing in the sweet Texas air. Well Ruby, who had been worried that I might be too much of a Yankee to fit in down there in Texas, had absolutely no idea why I was doing what I was doing, and why I was doing it on her watch. She stared at me incredulously as a look of rage started to appear in her eyes.

"What do you mean...you're "BREATHING THE AIR??" Ruby asked me incredulously, not really expecting an answer.

We were in her state now, she was on her way home, and there was no way I was privileged enough to stop and breathe any of her Texas air. Ruby, though she would forever argue to the contrary, was not, nor would ever be an artist. Ruby did not see the art nor the beauty in the Sun-kissed landscape of her own home state. Ruby did not see the beauty in the moment, Ruby did not see the beauty of breathing the air. Ruby was on her way home, and this was her state, not mine, I was not to bask in its Sun nor breathe its air, at least not for the sole purpose of pleasure. Ruby shook her head, bewildered, and stormed back to her car.

I was really hoping that Ruby was going to find happiness in Texas. It was and still is and forever shall be no mystery that New York makes people crazy and makes crazy people die. Hell, I met most of 'em. Ruby was no different than the rest of 'em and sanity remained elusive. From that point when we first met, to this point, far from its confines, far from the New York craziness, its filth and insanity, far from its death-sucking-on-death, Ruby finally stood her chance to unwind and find happiness. Ruby was finally in the place where she could take a deep breath, look around, and slow down a bit. No one would be following her down here, giving her shit, people wouldn't dislike her so much, people wouldn't fear her honesty and Ruby would be able to live in peace.

This was the place we chose to hunker down, and live a more boring life, but I was starting to get a strange feeling that Ruby, well Ruby may not be able to be as happy here as she had hoped. I was getting ahead of myself, though, we were still a couple of hundred miles from Rigler, she would cool out once we got there. Ruby's just looking for a home, Ruby's looking for the home she never had, and I knew we would find it once we got there. Come on, Rigler, don't let us down.

***

People, well people are basically assholes. People will fuck you any way they can, and the funny thing, shit the ironic thing is that it's usually friends and family that'll fuck you first. The world is a big pit filled with animals that call themselves human, call themselves civilized, but that's just how they want to see it. These animals are all trying to get on top of one another, both physically and otherwise. The majority of those that call themselves human are so fucking insecure that they can't even look in the mirror without having to have someone stand next to 'em for comparison. They have to fuck their neighbor or fuck their neighbor's wife so that their own mirror image is stronger by contrast.

People are all insecure little children in grown-up bodies, all trying to be the King of the Hill. It's funny though, that when you look at strangers, usually you're no threat to strangers, usually your mere presence doesn't threaten strangers, so they tend to leave you alone. Friends and family though, they're too close, they see you, you threaten 'em just by being, and they got to keep you down. Every unhappy moron's got to be King of his own hill, King of his own hill, or if he doesn't like his, he'll steal yours just to push you off and climb to the top of it. Why? Because it was there...because you're hill is taller than mine and I want your hill.

Ruby's family was funny in a sad sort of way. None of 'em, absolutely none of 'em...brothers, cousins, parents, uncles, aunts, absolutely none of 'em had anything whatsoever to do with any of the rest of 'em. Now we're talking an extended family of maybe sixty plus people, and within that circle, absolutely not one single one of 'em would have anything to do with any other one of 'em. There were times I saw this as extremely dysfunctional, and other times it just seemed pure and honest, not like Connecticut where you were supposed to like one another, just because that was the way it was supposed to be.

***

Dysfunctional...Shit...Pop Psychology with media-created political correctness... "Dysfunctional" means shit. I guess it's a way for people to define their fucked-up families and reach out and realize that there are other fucked-up families, and so forth and so on. "Co-dependent" is another marvel of modern verbiage. Basically, all the psychologists, the new religion came up with a term so people would feel like they were all in the same boat with everyone else. "Co-dependent" is a term that defines any relationship between any people living in this society, unless you're a hermit living up in the mountains with only your dog to talk to, which to a psychologist would be an "Inter-Species Co-Dependent Relationship".

I guess people in this world need definitions, they need words, 'cause they can't describe what's going on in their lives, so they read about it, coin the phrase, and go on talking about all their Co-dependent, Dysfunctional families. That way they know it's okay to be fucked-up, because everyone else is, too. Ruby however was from a truly fucked-up family, above and beyond any that has previously been researched or documented. There hadn't been a textbook yet written...

Back in Connecticut, it's weird, people aren't Dysfunctional, people are normal. My brother back in Connecticut used to keep telling me that he and his family were "normal". Well, the family was normal with the exclusion of me. I was from the same family, but I was way far from normal. I guess my brother was excluding me while describing the virtues of our family. I have always hated the idea of normalcy or conformity, but admitted it though, and as we all know, admitting a problem is the first step toward recovery...

Me, I moved to New York, I was too emotional, and I was too sensitive. I did bad things and I had the audacity to admit it. I didn't lie and cover up all of the abnormality in my life. Leaving home in my twenties was the icing on the cake. Back then and back there in Connecticut was like living on popcorn and having cotton candy and telling everyone, *"Have a Nice Day!"* And back there and back then, when they said, "Have a Nice Day!" they really meant it. It was really weird.

***

Yes, Ruby was far from normal, but I hadn't met many people I'd call normal, and those that did call themselves normal, really weren't. Perhaps "normal" was the Connecticut term for happy, well adjusted, perhaps it meant positive, I dunno. Ruby, on the other hand, was one of the most negative people I ever had known. I used to accept that it was the fault of her father, and the demons he left inside of her. She seemed to know what went wrong. On a clear day, Ruby would admit she was damaged and that she needed help, she knew why things were the way they were, and what should be done, but try to make that first appointment, try to get her to walk out that door.

The day finally came and Ruby had cooled out. She knew it was time to go, and I made the appointment for her. We had a good quiet meal together. I poured her a glass of wine and we joked around. She smiled in the dancing candlelight and seemed quite relaxed. We finished our dinner and after a while, Ruby seemed calm enough to go through with it. As we headed for the door and I turned out the light, all of a sudden, in a blind fury of rage, Ruby went into a fur-flying frenzy. She screamed with the hatred that had built up for years.

"YOU'RE THE ONE WHO'S CRAZY...I'M NOT CRAZY... WHO THE HELL DO YOU THINK YOU ARE MAKING THIS APPOINTMENT FOR ME?? CRAZY PEOPLE GO TO THESE THINGS. I'M NOT CRAZY! YOU ARE THE ONE WHO IS CRAZY! WHO DO YOU THINK YOU ARE TRYING TO TAKE ME TO A DOCTOR, ANYWAY? I FUCKING HATE YOU!!!"

Ruby started throwing fists like her life depended on it.

There comes a point when an adult has to start acting like an adult. There's a time when it doesn't matter what Daddy did to her, there comes a time when you have to grow out of it. Ruby never did grow out of it, Ruby just kept on leaving. Ruby kept on leaving so she wouldn't have to stay, so she wouldn't have to stay and face things, face herself and see her own face in the mirror. I guess I was hoping that her leaving would help her leave the demons behind her, but time went on I saw the only thing that kept leaving was Ruby.

***

I remember opium. It's funny, at the time I didn't remember opium, but years later, looking back, I remember opium.

It was in the days before Corporate Amerika turned everything into predictable, marketable, cheap and available crack cocaine. There had been a variety of substances over the years, and things were good. There was a greater variety, and there were more soft drugs in those days before the major proliferation of white powders and small plastic vials of rock. Slick Rick and me were hanging out, it was just before he went into the Navy, and we were tearing it up real good, for old time's sake. I don't think they had the piss test in those days, but if they did, it was pretty obvious that Rick really didn't care.

I remember the stash me and Rick had that summer, the one I called the Summer of Bliss. For whatever reason, he and me had both, separately stored the best of various stashes from the past year or so, and what he didn't have, I did, and what I didn't have, he did. Amazing shit it was. There was opium, honey oil, black beauties, lines, fresh 'shrooms picked daily by a Brother who lived off-campus, and blotter, pure and strong blotter fresh all the time from

MIT. Blotters with circles the size of quarters, and damn, those engineers in those days knew how to throw some shit together, and twelve hours later, you couldn't really think much about coming down, 'cause by then you forgot what coming down was all about. It was better living through chemistry.

So me and Rick saved the best of the best and there we were a couple of days before he was going into Basic Training, and we saved the opium and the honey oil for that particular time in history. Man, the shit was amazing…

I don't remember how it started, but I remember the both of us, laying flat on our backs, somehow in communion, looking up at that intricate God that at other times would have looked like the ceiling. I closed my eyes briefly, and when I opened 'em up, we were both in Red's Roadhouse, out in the middle of nowhere. I was knocking the shit out of this video game, and the score was high enough that it made me think that we'd been there for a while.

"Rick!" I hollered over the roar of the band, "what game is this??"

"Asteroids!" he hollered back.

"Far out! How did we get here??"

"You drove!"

"Shit!" I roared at the brief glimpse of reality before I went back to playing my game.

***

Ruby was kind of like opium. There were times there was euphoria, pure and ecstatic, but there were times, more times than not when I'd stop, open my eyes, look around, and ask, *"where the fuck am I, and how did I get here?"*

***

Ruby just kept on leaving, and at that point in her life, she chose to take me with her. Ruby was from a military family, which got her used to moving every year of her life. Later on, I found out that her Mother's mother was Gypsy, none of which helped Ruby find any solace in staying still for very long. There was also Ruby running from her demons, running so scared she just knew that if she kept on moving they couldn't catch up with her, they just couldn't, she wouldn't let them. So she took me with her for a while, just so long as we didn't stay still for very long. She was the leavinest gal I ever knew, and for those couple of years we were together, I guess I was just as leavin' as she was.

Like I've said, Ruby just couldn't be happy. Ruby longed for stability in her quiet moments, but ridiculed the stability I had come from. She longed for sweet-eyed naive boys who hadn't yet become molesters, but the part of me that still had that Connecticut naiveté pissed the hell out of her, no one could be that innocent. On good days, she said she trusted me more than anyone but would always come around to challenge me and to search for that one shred of doubt that would prove I was as dishonest as the rest of 'em. She tried as hard as she could to prove that I was just like the rest of those dishonest, corrupting men.

I had hoped that Texas would help her relax and slow down a bit. New York's enough to drive anyone nuts, and sometimes the nuts just gotta leave New York to see if they will ever stand a chance.

***

We arrived in Rigler, Texas on a warm autumn day. It was December but the Sun was warm and high. It was worlds away from New York, and I was so sick of East Coast winters, that I felt we had found the right place to be. For myself, I knew there was no turning back. The Texas Sun was smiling at me, and I smiled back. I was glad Ruby would finally have a safe place to live and to find her happiness.

We pulled up in front of the house on Parish Street in our modern wagon train with the still-warm breeze blowing through the bare autumn trees. We stood there in the modest housing development that sat on the outskirts of town, surrounded by horses and longhorns grazing in the rolling grassy hills. The house was a quaint brick ranch on a fenced-in half acre. It was a fairly modern house that rested under a canape of shade trees with a lovely pecan tree in the backyard. It looked real nice to me, but immediately Ruby was finding all the flaws. The place hadn't been properly cleaned, no one had told us we had to go down to the utility company to have everything turned on, and how were we gonna maintain all that lawn, and who was gonna rake the leaves?

I assured Ruby that none of these things were insurmountable and that I would take care of everything, but that wasn't good enough. Someone was fucking us over, and someone was fucking poor Ruby over again, and it was fast looking doubtful that she'd be happy here, too.

Ruby spent the next several days on her hands and knees, scrubbing and used bleach to clean in-between the bathroom tiles and she cleaned each and every window with a razor blade. In the evenings she would complain about how much work she had to do because no one else would do it.

Over the next couple of weeks, we got the house in good condition, bought some furniture, and it looked like things were gonna be okay after all. Ruby however, spent most of her time looking back at how much she was being fucked over again, and complained too much about all the work she had to do an' such, but in all of her new-found misery, not once could she just get into the moment, sit back and relax, and look around and appreciate her nice clean, new house.

***

We registered the cars, toured the town and found out what needed to be found out. Months passed and Lizzie wouldn't start school until the spring and we would have the entire winter to relax and regroup. Except Ruby.

Ruby was rushing around like everything had to happen on the spot. Everything was priority and only Ruby could organize it properly. The lawn couldn't be mowed next week, it had to mowed today, but we didn't have a lawn mower. Ruby was in a major frenzy over what to do about things. Lizzie and me wanted to go to the lake, but Ruby wouldn't hear of it. There was too much to do and going to the lake just didn't fit into Ruby's plans.

Slowly it seemed that Ruby was getting things under control and we finally took some time off and went to the lake north of Duncanville, in Oklahoma, over the Red River. We brought a picnic and had a pleasant day. Lizzie and Ruby had a good time that day. Ruby was starting to relax. They seemed to be close, but usually Ruby was in too much of a frenzy to have any quiet time with anyone, even Lizzie. That day Ruby and Lizzie waded in the lake and played together and talked and laughed well into the afternoon. They walked off together, arm in arm, giggling like a couple of schoolgirls. Ruby was young when she had Lizzie, and still retained her youthful appearance. They could have been sisters. It was like two best friends that day, Lizzie and Ruby sharing secrets and telling jokes. They both seemed calm and contented and I was seeing that being out of New York was finally gonna make a world of difference in the way things were gonna be. Ruby smiled the whole day long.

***

We had a few good days, driving around, touring places from Ruby's youth, but Ruby started mentioning the evil, that there was always some evil, some insidious menace that was lurking just below the surface, everywhere we went.

I asked Ruby when she wanted to visit her favorite uncle, Lem Grady. Ruby had not stopped talking about Uncle Lem and how he was her favorite uncle and the best one of the Grady clan. I kept asking but Ruby kept putting it off to the point where I wasn't sure if she even wanted to see him after all.

Although she kept talking about it, we didn't go back to the cemetery to see the family gravesite either. As time went on, Ruby got annoyed if I mentioned it. We finally drove out there once. I thought it was a real shame that the gravesite had fallen into disrepair and was so overgrown with grass and weeds, but Ruby had no further interest in fixing it up and it wasn't discussed again.

Ruby got a job the second week we were there, a fairly high paying office job. High paying jobs were scarce in that small town, and she was quite pleased...for about two or three days. After her first week of work, Ruby was pissed off again. There was a woman in the office she said was jealous of her, and her boss was a pain in the ass. I asked her if she ever had a boss who wasn't a pain in the ass, and she said that this just goes to show that the male Conspiracy permeated everything everywhere. She was upset because people like her boss had seeped even down here to Rigler, and had ruined the place of her birth. It hadn't been like this when she was a girl.

I thought about New York and I started to see the same behavior coming back. The demons were slowly raising their head, just in the periphery of Ruby's awareness. We had come all this way, all this way out to this beautiful place, far from the maddening crowd, far from the noise, far from the diseased air, far from the insanity and Ruby still wasn't satisfied.

***

The more Ruby did, the more she got depressed. When she met people or reunited with someone from her past, she would find that there was an uncle in the Pen, or a grandmother who had died slowly. One day at the diner, we saw someone she had talked about as a long lost friend from high school. Ruby just shied away, knowing that only disaster and more deceit would come from any further reunions. She spent increasingly more time in the house or in the backyard, not wanting to come out. The evil was back and the demons had finally settled back in.

Work wasn't treating her much better, either. She saw the politics and favoritism and would come home, weaving the threads into her larger male Conspiracy theory. Ruby would lose sleep at night, trying to figure out how to make things right, how to make the evil ones go away.

Ruby had become quiet in those days. She didn't lose it and get loud like she did back there in New York. She would spend most of her time in a slow-burning funk, not knowing what to do. Her demons started coming back, caressing her with fond memories of her childhood in Rigler and how it had all gone to shit. She was constantly being reminded of how men had fucked-up one more thing in her life.

***

It was quiet but it was depressing. Everything everyone had ever said about "coming home again" was starting to sink into Ruby's fragile demeanor. Instead of learning, instead of becoming older and wiser, Ruby sank even deeper into the realization that she had no home and never would. In New York, Ruby had been everything from a lover to an adversary, but here, here in Rigler, Ruby was more like a presence, a sad and enduring presence, devoid of most emotion except that of depression.

***

Ruby started noticing things, little things, but little things that hinted of a greater evil of which we were not fully aware. She would come home and swear that the furniture had been moved, not noticeably, but ever so slightly. A picture hanging on the wall had been minutely shifted, just to catch her attention. One day she got into her car after work and noticed that the position of the drivers seat had been shifted, almost unnoticeable, just so she would know. She had to be made aware. I didn't quite know what she was talking about, but she insisted that the Conspiracy had finally found out about her presence there in Rigler. She knew that they knew that she was there to spread goodness and to defeat the evil that proliferated.

Nothing had been unlocked, or left unlocked, there was no sign of forced entry, and there was no obvious sign of anything being tampered with, but Ruby knew. Ruby knew they were following her and ever-so-slightly, giving her ever-so-subtle warnings about what they could do to her.

Ruby swore that there were no signs of forced entry and nothing left obvious, because they knew of her sharp sense, they knew she was psychic, and she knew who they all were, or she would find out soon enough. They didn't have to knock her door down, Ruby had the fragile threshold of reality planted firmly in her mind, and anything out of the ordinary was obvious to her. Ruby was no fool and she said they did it just to show her that they could. That was all it was…just little, subtle, almost unnoticeable things happening at the threshold level of dangerous threatening that would keep her in her place.

***

Ruby started seeing more and more of the Conspiracy's web of deceit. She saw housewives, enslaved by the valium their husbands kept feeding 'em. She knew the pharmacist was in on it, and figured it was probably related to the larger drug smuggling conspiracy. She knew that those housewives had probably been as pure as she had been, but they knew too much, and their innate goodness was too much of a threat to the good ol' boys who were gonna keep 'em down.

The more she looked around, the more evil she saw. She knew of the evil of the world, and she knew that she was the messenger, the messenger to save what innocence there was left, but it was not no supposed to happen here, not in Rigler, Texas. Here she was in the town of her birth, the last place where she had known innocence and simplicity, many years before, and here she found the Conspiracy, fucking things up like they had everywhere else. Ruby was getting increasingly pissed off.

Ruby was rapidly going from depressed to pissed off. She wasn't gonna let it happen here, not in Rigler. Ruby started wondering when this all happened. She knew it wasn't like this when she was a little girl. She knew even back then, in all her innocence, they wouldn't dare commit these acts. She knew everything was good and pure when she was a little girl, and she knew it was because of her own purity. It must have happened after she left, that was the only time they would have had the opportunity to get together and figure the whole thing out.

Ruby had lived in Rigler one more time after her childhood, her last year of high school. She looked back and thought. She remembered kids getting high and figured that was the beginning of it. The Conspiracy's goal was to enslave as many as they could, but they had to start slowly, they couldn't be noticed. Getting everyone high was a good start. It was blackmail pure and simple. If they got everyone high, then they could hold it over their heads like a carrot on a stick, and then they would have the slaves they needed to do the dirty work. It was so simple Ruby couldn't believe she had missed it the first time, but here she was older and wiser, and Ruby now knew why we were back in Rigler.

Ruby said we needed guns. We couldn't allow this to go on any longer. At least for self-defense we needed guns, maybe a lot of guns. Ruby said we may have to go in and take care of things if things got too out of hand, but for now we needed guns for self-defense. Ruby said I wasn't to buy them anywhere in the county, that would tip 'em off that we were armed and ready. The Conspiracy ran wide and the farther away we went, the less they would know. They were already sending her subtle, ever so subtle threats, so we couldn't push our luck anymore. From now on our plans had to be kept secret.

We would take walks late in the night, we couldn't talk in the house anymore, Ruby knew they had bugged it, and could hear everything we thought or said. From now on, we were at war, and the easiest way to win was to keep the enemy away from the knowledge we had.

The next week I toured the pawnshops of Fort Worth and found a couple of good concealment weapons. I also picked up an old cowboy six-shooter, a single-action Colt .45, just for the hell of it. It was a nice collectible, probably not that efficient in terms of technology, but with hollow points, it left holes about an inch wide in a thick sheet of metal and that seemed good enough to me. I bought Ruby a straightforward .38 Chief's Special, figuring that that could take care of any mess she needed to clean up. Me, I looked a bit harder. I went from pawnshop to pawnshop, knowing there was one out there for me. I finally found her, that beautiful stainless 5-shot .380 semi-auto, laying there in the display case in front of me, smiling up at me. I looked down through that glass shelf and smiled back. It was that simple.

***

We moved out of the place in town after a couple of months. Ruby just couldn't settle in there, even after we cleaned it up and made it livable, she just couldn't forget what a mess it was in when we first moved in and it was too close to where everyone would know what she was up to.

I found that place out in Brahma Meadows, out in the county, well past the city limits. It was ten wooded acres in the middle of nowhere. It was nestled in some rolling green hills, spotted with the red clay, from where the Red River got its name. We were several miles from our nearest neighbor, past several ranches, off a gravel road, off a gravel road. The gravel driveway was about a quarter-mile long, and we could basically do whatever we wanted. We could burn trash, shoot guns, and piss wherever we wanted. Clothing was optional. Ruby started loosening up. There were times when Lizzy was away, when Ruby would walk out the back door wearing just a pair of shorts, smiling, with her large, firm breasts shining in the Texas sunlight.

I had never seen her quite so relaxed and figured that maybe we should have just gotten the fuck away from people from the start. Lizzie seemed like she was getting bored and by that time she was approaching sixteen and there were no sixteen-year-old boys for miles, Lizzie seemed like she was bored most of the time. Overall though, it was as quiet and removed as you could get. My only concern was that I worked the graveyard shift at the diner over in Rigler and leaving the two women alone in the middle of nowhere bothered me a bit.

Ruby had no problem learning to shoot. We had already bought the guns, and she remembered once in a while that it was best to know how to use 'em. Lizzie wanted no part of guns. I tried to tell her that target shooting was a good thing to know, and that she didn't ever have to shoot anyone if she didn't want, but she was distant. Lizzie was not Ruby and did not share Ruby's concerns about things that were going on.

Texas is great…after dinner, your host and his wife go around the house and show you all the guns, one under each side of the bed, two in the closet, one behind the commode, just in case. People in Texas had guns all over the place and people in Texas are damn proud of their guns.

***

I came home from work that night, early morning actually, about Three-thirty, to find Ruby out in the driveway, wearing nothing but shorts and cowboy boots, holding the .45 in both hands, shooting determined, into the woods. The scene seemed perfectly normal to me, but I thought I'd ask anyway. Ruby said there was a pack of wild dogs, or coyote, or something, that came to take the puppy away. I went into the kitchen for a cold beer. No big deal. After all, a woman's gotta have a hobby.

I came home that other night, nothing outa the ordinary. It was some time before four in the morning as I walked into the kitchen from the driveway. I stumbled around the kitchen, got a beer, and made a sandwich. I probably killed about thirty minutes before I went into the bedroom. I opened the door, and there in front of me was Ruby. She was sitting up in bed, back to the wall, with that .45 firmly held in both hands. *"Is that you?"* she called out. I didn't know who she meant, but replied, *"It's Dave!"* hoping that was the desired response. She let out a deep sigh and put the pistol down. She said she'd asked out loud several times when she heard all the banging around in the kitchen, but apparently I hadn't heard her. I assumed it wasn't me she was planning to shoot. All I really know for sure is that that Ruby was holding that big ol' .45 lookin' me right in the face in that dark room that night.

Overall, things were pretty good. Ruby didn't like her job that much, but coming home, back to that house at night, helped to separate her from the rest of the world and its madness. We both worked different shifts and that seemed to be the one main ingredient for our marital bliss. We saw each other a couple of hours each day, usually on the run, and that was good.

***

After about a month at the new place, Ruby started noticing things, subtle things, but things nonetheless. We lived on Riker Trail, and Ruby knew Kyle Riker was one of the villains back there in Rigler. Not wanting anything to slip by her, Ruby went to the County Courthouse and researched the area. Sure enough, Riker Trail was named after Kyle Riker's grandfather, who had owned a ranch out there, maybe forty years prior. Ruby knew that land in Texas didn't change hands that often, and that if we were out there, then Kyle Riker surely knew about it. Ruby started speaking in whispered tones, and asked me to take long walks with her down that long gravel road.

Ruby wasn't sure if they had been in the house yet, but she knew that sooner or later, they'd be taping our conversations, listening in. Nothing would be confidential in our house any more.

Ruby asked me to buy more bullets, she said we couldn't be too sure any more, and it was better to be safe than sorry. I wasn't to buy the bullets anywhere in the county, even at the Walmart, she knew that was too close, they would find out that we were getting ready.

I drove about thirty miles south and bought about five hundred rounds of assorted bullets for all the guns, all wad-cutters or hollow-points, it was better to be safe than sorry. Ruby started target shooting with a vengeance, out in the back yard, almost every day. She made sure that the .38 was loaded and ready, under the seat of her car at all times. I told her that might get her in trouble if she ever got stopped speeding or whatever. Ruby told me that she knew the cops were in on it too, and that no one was gonna get her to step outa the car at any time. By this point, that made enough sense to me, mostly because I wasn't about to argue with her anyway.

***

Ruby started to suspect that they had planted bugs at her job, too. She found out that Kyle Riker's cousin owned the security company that wired the alarm system at work. She knew that was too close for comfort, and next to guns and land, that family was the biggest thing in Texas. If Kyle Riker knew about Ruby's plans, then his cousin was sure to help put a stop to her plans.

One day Ruby had me climb up a stepladder at work, up into the drop ceiling over the office after hours, asking me if I saw anything that looked suspicious. I looked around, flashlight in hand, but couldn't see a damned thing. I told her that everything looked okay, but she said that only went to show how sophisticated the technology had become. When I came to visit her at work, Ruby insisted that we only converse outside the building, and in whispered tones.

Ruby spent most of her time plotting and planning the fall of the Conspiracy. She took me on long walks down the gravel road, where they couldn't listen in. She knew we could take them all out if we did it right. It would be difficult, but she knew we could do it. They were evil and didn't deserve to remain on this planet.

She made sure we had enough bullets and that there was a gun in each car and several in the house. We weren't to talk about it in the house or on the phone. Ruby knew they were on their way in and it was just us against them, it would be self-defense, pure and simple.

***

Ruby wasn't sleeping well. She kept hearing things outside, all times of day. She started sleeping with the .38 under her pillow, hammer cocked. The .45 was too big and too hard to rapid-fire. Ruby knew we were starting to face an all-or-nothing situation, and she wanted to be ready.

Ruby was starting to get depressed in a big way. I thought it was from the lack of sleep, but as time went on, it seemed that her nerves were getting severely shot from all the details they were taking in. Ruby started looking everywhere in the house for signs of the ever-growing Conspiracy, but just couldn't find any physical evidence. She knew it was there, she just couldn't find it.

Things started going wrong at Ruby's job. She wouldn't talk to too many people, and usually reserved conversations for outside of the building. She started researching who was related to who and what the women's maiden names were. Ruby became increasingly depressed as she learned of all the connections she had failed to notice from the start. Although she knew it was the men who were behind the Conspiracy, she was starting to notice wives, ex-wives, sisters, daughters, aunts and cousins, who all had some involvement. Ruby was convinced that the women were slaves, beholden to the men out of necessity, but they still couldn't be trusted. When Ruby found out who had a drinking problem or which one was on valium, she knew that was how the Conspiracy kept them all in line.

***

Ruby had her plans, and noble plans they were. She knew good must triumph over evil, and the power of right was what was gonna keep us on to… that and several hundred rounds of ammunition.

Ruby started really dragging. She stayed up most nights, going over and over the plan in her mind. Every day she was different, every day she was slipping, lower and lower, sinking into the abyss. She stopped talking to me and Lizzie, and many times we would find her outside, sitting there alone in tears. She didn't want to talk about it, but I strongly suspected that the Conspiracy had gotten to her.

As time went on, there was no one Ruby wanted to socialize with or even talk to anymore. Although we were miles out of Rigler, way out in the county, Ruby knew they were always watching us. She stopped going outside and usually kept the curtains drawn. It was a downward spiral and I wasn't sure how much longer it could go on. I was thinking that the best thing to do was to get everyone out of Rigler, out of Texas, and hope that moving on would help to clear things up.

I'd always liked New Mexico and it wasn't that far, now that we were that far from New York. I couldn't imagine Ruby getting into too much trouble that far out in the Southwestern desert, and decided that it was my turn to make the decision, and I went and told Ruby and Lizzie that that was what we were gonna do.

THE LAST JOURNEY

Some people, well some people say, *"don't sink to their level,"* when dealing with others. Some people think they're better than others, and just by being smarter or more educated, or richer, or whatever, that they can solve any problem just by being them, and by not *"sinking to another's level."*

Regis Ryan was a friend of a friend and used to always talk about "the workers" or "the plight of the American Negro", and was concerned about Third-World suffering but never lost any sleep over any of it and the sonofabitch had never worked a day in his life, and if he'd ever even met one, no self-respecting American Negro would have had anything to do with him. Regis was intelligent but not very smart, he could only adapt to environments that had already been laid-out for him. The unpredictable or the unknown were territories where he could not tread.

Since I left Connecticut, I was usually the only Glow-In-The-Dark, so I've had to rely on a variety of survival tactics. The ability to kick ass was a powerful one, though if you carried it right, you never had to use it, but you got the ghetto respect that kept you walking on down that sidewalk late at night. The other, the more important ability, was the ability to become invisible, to blend in, dropping the energy to such a low level, no one really noticed you. Either way, back when I lived out in Bed Stuy, Brooklyn, they either respected me, put up with me, or just didn't see me, but I never ran into any serious shit, until Regis was around.

Regis was a friend of a friend, and inevitably, halfway down Fulton Street, heading for the "A" Train, you'd start to hear, *"Fuck You, Honkie!"* and similar epithets of disrespect. The Spades would fuck with us left and right, but me, walking alone in that same hood at any other time, never had one incident of aggression. The point was that Regis couldn't speak the language, walk the walk, and none of them there on Fulton Street could give a good Holy Goddamn about the Plight of the American Negro. Regis wouldn't "sink to their level" and with all of his academic ramblings on the subject, couldn't even face it when he was faced with it. There were times I thought it'd be fun to leave poor Regis there, alone on Fulton Street, to have his own liberal experience in the ghetto.

Me, I look at it as communicating with people on a level that they can understand. *"Don't sink to their level"* is an example of Christian judgment and Connecticut condescension. Who is to say that their level is "sunken"? It's merely a different level, and since we are all animals with no hope of ever evolving, perhaps those condescending Christians are the ones whose level is sunken.

So me, I like to communicate efficiently and to be understood. There's no sense wasting time in these matters. If *"fuck you, asshole"* gets the message across, then why waste time with the Webster's in one hand and white guilt in the other. Communicate, get the point across, and move on...

***

Since only the weapons have evolved, I now have my highly evolved .380 so I can communicate with those who live on that level. No judgment, just understanding one another on a different level. The only thing humans have to understand one another is communication, however poor a medium that may be.

***

I had a feeling that Ruby was gone. Going back to Rigler had been a complete failure and it didn't take long for her to realize that she had to leave again. People got wise to her quickly in Rigler and like everywhere else, they feared her honesty and her goodness, they knew she had come in to clean things up, and the time came when she knew it was time to leave. This time I decided to call the shots, and we ended up in the desert hills outside of Albuquerque. I had to get Ruby as far away from people and as far away from Rigler as possible.

I had wanted to leave several times before, and a few times I made the phone calls and made the plans in my head, but in the long run, I figured that our brief time together wasn't enough to give up yet. As far as I had come from Connecticut, I couldn't shake the notion that everything could be worked out with love.

I don't know if I ever really loved Ruby. I didn't even like the idea of love, that sweet notion had been dead long ago. Too many imposters along the way will suck it right out of you and years down the road, people had to wonder if there was still anything left. I think at that point I had seen love as a conscious decision. Love didn't just fall from the sky anymore, but I didn't see that as a bad thing. Hell, Ruby didn't even love herself, so she couldn't even know what she was missing. I had a feeling that things were over, but wasn't ready to put it into my consciousness yet. I remember driving out into the desert that day just to savor my aloneness and it wasn't bad at all. I was enjoying her being gone. I was enjoying the idea of finally being without her and her pain, without her drama and her agony. I was sick of her demons who kept finding her, and sick of trying to help her to move on without 'em. The demons might have come in unannounced and uninvited, but at that point in her life, Ruby knew they were there, why they were there, and knew how to get rid of 'em, but Ruby was blissful in her agony, and chose to let 'em stay. Between Ruby and me, and all of her demons, our bed had gotten much too small.

***

It takes the right amount of coffee and tobacco to get in the right mood these days. Not necessarily a good mood, but the Mood. I guess it used to be coke and a lot of alcohol, but that mood usually resulted in a lotta mournful lethargy, nothing ever really got done and not being habitual, I would always pay the price the next day. You need the Mood, with the energy, with the ambition, to figure it all out. I prefer it these days, some coffee and some cigarette... controlled anger is much more pleasurable than diffused anger. If you're gonna be really pissed off, you should make sure you can shoot straight.

***

We found a nice frame house on the outskirts of Albuquerque, facing the western desert. Sandia Peak, glowing red from the sunset, rose in the east. It was a nice little house with a small, fenced-in yard, but Ruby was dissatisfied. She spent the first week, cleaning and complaining that she would never live in a nice modern house. Everything was filthy. She was destined to spend eternity on her hands and knees, scrubbing someone else's house. I didn't even try to comfort her. No answer, no amount of comforting would have been enough.

The neighbors came and went. They worked day jobs and Ruby was concerned that they didn't wave as they passed. Surely they were hiding something. Ruby tried to concentrate on what it was they all held in communion, that they were hiding from us. Ruby knew something was going on and the neighbors all knew that it had to be kept from her. Ruby was goodness and that would surely put a stop to their plans.

Ruby spent several days, deep in thought, concerned that she was the one who had to figure out what new evil surrounded us, even out there in the desert, nothing was pure. She still hung on to the thread of a hope that the Conspiracy had not yet permeated every square inch of ground she would someday walk on, but that thread was fast eroding.

By the end of the first week, Ruby felt well enough to go for a drive into town. A few miles from the house, she slammed on the brakes and pulled over to the side of the road. She was pale and choked up. I asked her what was wrong. *"LOOK!"* was all she said. I looked up and saw a house for sale and asked her what the problem was. *"L-look again!"* she stuttered. I surveyed the house, the yard, and finally my gaze froze on the realtor's sign. "House For Sale - Call Riker Realty." The Conspiracy had finally found Ruby. There was no longer any place to hide.

***

Lizzie was having a miserable time in Albuquerque. I had never seen that poor girl have such a hard time. Being Ruby's daughter, Lizzie had had to live in a lot of places over the years. Wherever she lived, Lizzie had always made friends and had a good time for a teenage girl. Albuquerque was full of gang bangers and a lot of white wanna-be's, every bit of gangsta learned from watching teevee and it seemed that every little shithead who got thrown out of school anywhere else in America was relocated to Albuquerque for "a fresh start". Lizzie found herself surrounded by drugs, guns and spoiled rich boy attitude… it was teenage hell.

Wages were low in Albuquerque, and it was fast becoming obvious that nothing there would make us rich. Ruby decided to take Lizzie back to Rigler to see if they could get something new going there. I found out about the Town Grille becoming available, and wanted Ruby to look into that for me. Ruby had already fucked up and lost her job managing the retail store. She was making a fair salary, but just couldn't hang on any longer. Everything was closing in on her, and I was the one left with a job. I stayed behind, because I had the paycheck, but at that point I wasn't too sure about following Ruby any more. Buying the Town Grille may have been the answer to all we needed or it may have been just something else.

Ruby was leaving a second time to Texas, and this time it seemed different, and I wondered that if she was drawn to it that much, then maybe it was the place for her. Maybe that was a good sign. Ruby knew what we left behind there in Rigler and maybe she was now prepared to face it without fear or illusion. Maybe Ruby was finally finding a place to call home.

Ruby was looking for a fresh start, and said that she wanted to be "Valerie" now. Her grandmother's name was Valerie, and for some time, Ruby realized she wasn't getting by as Ruby. She couldn't control who Ruby was, and she figured that being Valerie just might lead her to a safer place. I told her she could be Valerie, she could be anyone she wanted. At this point I was getting pretty fed up with who Ruby was, too. I was more and more realizing that Ruby was just a thin mask over a deep sea of depression and negativity, and I was fast coming to that point where I couldn't deal with it any more.

***

I guess the biggest difference between me and Ruby was that she'd preach all of this perceived morality, and how she knew how the world could be a better place, but would always slip back into being a negative and belligerent pain in the ass. I lived, breathed, and acted the same morality that I always had. If she acted the way she talked, then everything would have been okay. Ruby had to make all those fanatical pronouncements in order to kid herself that she was the only moral and decent one left, and for maybe my first year with her I actually believed it. Ruby's preaching wore thin, and what I soon came to realize was that she was preaching so loud, because she was preaching to the lack of morality that dwelled within herself.

The demons had been eating away at her since such an early age, I had seen that all of her preaching came from the shell of a memory of who she once was and who she thought she could have been. All she had left was the shell of the memory of all that had been lost. I used to say that a person I could be with would be the one who found the hundred dollar bill they knew just fell out of that person's pocket, and return it. I used to think Ruby was that kind of person. As time went on I realized that she would have helped that person out of their hundred dollar bill, all the while continuing to preach about how low the human condition had sunk. To me the morality starts and ends with each individual. If you can't change the world, at least you can go home at peace with yourself.

Ruby however, would find slight inconsistencies in something I would say or do, and if there were none, she would create them, and show me what a horrible liar I was. She would blame me for having sex with other women before I had even met her. She knew I was a vile and evil person, and she knew her psychic abilities were telling her so. She could conjure up the images to prove her point. If she spent enough time alone with herself, she could conjure up all the evil necessary to prove her point. She was always swimming in the evidence that would help her start her next war.

***

A couple of days before Ruby left, she went into another rage, the cause of which is still unclear to me, but this was it, she was finally leaving me…again. I was not to come back to Rigler with her, this was it, it was finally over. Ruby hated me, Lizzie hated me, I was useless and I was evil, this was it, it was finally over. It was finally over about a month before we got married two years prior, it was over some time the year after that, and it seemed to be finally over again. It was a drama I had had dress rehearsal for time and time again, but I was quickly growing tired of her arrogance and aggression. I was tired of seeing an otherwise intelligent person repeating the same old stupid mistakes time and time again. The timing was fine. This time I was gonna let her leave, this time she was on her own.

Two days after her final proclamation, she wanted us all to go out as a family. She thought it would be nice to take a nice drive, walk through the mall and have dinner together, but by then I had had it. I was not about to go on perpetuating Ruby's fluctuating view of happiness. Ruby said she wanted us to go out as a family together, that she was sorry and everything could be okay now. All we had to do was go out together as a family and everything would be okay. I told Ruby that I couldn't go on with her fleeting contentment with sporadic family life. I told her I was tired of the way everything had been going, and that going to the mall and having dinner together was not even gonna begin taking care of the way things had become. She was acting out the very Connecticut Christian denial she had so vehemently decried, and I was not about to regress at this point. She wanted everything to be okay and everything to look fine on the surface, but by now I was tired of all the lies.

Ruby broke down again. She said she was tired of all the fighting and she said she wanted us to get a fresh start together back in Rigler. All the fighting had gone on long enough, and Ruby was now ready to make her peace. She cried in my arms, and finally admitted that she knew how fucked up she was, and how sorry she was that she had mistreated me so. I was the best she had ever had, and no one had ever taken such good care of her. Ruby just wanted everything to be all right. I had never seen her so sincere nor so remorseful. I felt a strength swelling from deep inside, and I held onto her and told her that yes, everything would be all right.

The next day we kissed in the driveway as Ruby and Lizzie drove off to Rigler to get the Town Grill deal started. She had my business plan and my credit cards and I looked forward to finally getting a fresh start together. I took a deep breath and went back inside the house.

**

Things were weird. There I was alone in the desert, glad she was gone, and at the same time glad we were gonna be together again. I was glad she had decided to start fresh, and I was glad she was finally admitting that she needed help. I was glad she was gonna give it a go. I guess she had tried to give it a fresh start in the past, but I looked at it as a process of elimination. How many more times could she leave? How many more times could she totter furiously, that close to the edge without spontaneously combusting?

There had been so many bad things we had left behind us. By process of elimination, I couldn't see too many more things that were left to let her down.

I had almost left her many times before. In my mind, I had already left. I had already left her with her daddy and her demons, and all the shit she brought with her, but then there was Lizzie. Lizzie was Ruby's daughter, but Lizzie was relatively unscathed by all the damage. She was a smart kid, a cute young girl and had started calling me "Dad" over the years. I taught her how to drive and would comfort her when Ruby went off the deep end. Lizzie deserved more, and there was the fact that our years together were just beginning, and all we had to do was work at it. If we worked at it, really worked at it, there would be nothing that could stop us...

***

I found his phone number on a piece of paper near the phone. Ruby hadn't even tried to conceal it. I dialed the number back in Rigler but hung up when I heard his voice. There wasn't much more I needed to know. After that, there didn't seem to be much need to stay in Albuquerque. There I was, sitting there in the middle of the fucking desert when the bills started rolling in. Motels in Corpus Christi, and Shreveport, and it was obvious that Ruby was getting around. I thought about her with that dumb yahoo she used to go with back in high school, and figured that this was the bottom she chose to sink to. I canceled all the credit cards. I couldn't sit tight. We had moved to Albuquerque because of all the people she thought were trying to kill her back in Rigler. I guess she returned 'cause no one was trying to kill her in New Mexico. If her wish did come true, then maybe there would be someone else back there, who would keep me from being the one going to jail.

So fuck all this sitting still, there was not much for me to do staying in Albuquerque. I thought about Lizzie, and my need to fulfill my obligation to her. I may as well say good-bye to her and provide for her one last time. It's not her fault about Ruby, and I didn't need all that stuff anyway. Furniture, appliances, whatever it was, it was now anchors to me, but stuff that would make Lizzie's life that much easier. I knew that Ruby couldn't provide for her, so I decided to go back to Texas and make one final gesture. Maybe two.

Loading the truck was a pain in the ass, but Charlie from the reservation and Brad helped me, so it didn't take all that much time, it was just hot as hell. I headed out around noon on that hot July day. Before I left, I called Lorna Brill back in Rigler. Now Lorna was a good ol' gal, she was a sophisticated, classy, big-haired pistol packin' mama, and sweet as she was, there was no one who would mess with her, knowing what she would do if she had to. I told Lorna that I'd be back in town the next day or so, but she was concerned about me driving all that way alone. I told her I'd pull over to stop and sleep if the going got rough.

Well Lorna knew I had my highly-evolved .380, and made me promise not to be without it, in that remote desert between Albuquerque and west Texas. I hadn't really thought about it, and everything I owned was in the truck, with my car in tow. The more I did think about it, the more I realized how smart it was to carry that pistol with me. It's a nice pistol, small and easily concealed, but it doesn't have a large capacity, so I bought an extra clip. Five rounds in each magazine and one in the chamber made it a compact six-shooter with five to spare. Eleven shots is not as many as some carry, but I got Right, and I got the power of the Lord with me so eleven is all I need.

***

     I slid that lovin' .380 into my pants pocket, climbed up into the Rent-a-Truck and headed out east into the hot New Mexico desert.

     The hot New Mexico Sun hit me hard, and fuck… I soon found out the air conditioning wasn't working. I knew I was gonna raise hell about it when I dropped the truck off there in Texas, but that didn't make it any more pleasant at the time. I only hoped I wouldn't get too pissed off on the way and didn't wanna waste any bullets before I got to Ruby.

     Out in the desert there is nothing but extremes...light and dark, hot and cold, life and death. There is no middle ground, no excuses. In that respect it reminded me a lot of New York. The desert has a funny way of cutting through the bullshit and helping you to forget this civilized and modern world. All of a sudden, in the middle of nowhere, truck or no truck, you're primitive with all the impulses, emotions and instincts to survive and to endure. It became increasingly obvious why the Indians in the Southwest were so spiritual. There are times when it's hard to tell the heavens from the earth, it all becomes one. In that high desert, at that altitude, I couldn't exactly see where the land ended and where the sky began. I saw the mountains, early in the morning, rising high above the tops of the clouds, and in a while, in that oxygen-shy altitude you realize that the differences don't really matter any more.

     Years before, in Acid-induced elevation, I could see that there was something else, but I couldn't ever tell exactly what. Acid left me with the awareness of what things weren't, but didn't ever tell me what things really were. Acid was a starting point that led me to that desert with its harsh extremes and a true sense of the connection between the Earth and the Spirit.

When Ruby an' Lizzie an' me were coming out from Rigler, before all this shit hit the fan, it was usually me in the lead, me driving the truck with Ruby and Lizzie following behind in Ruby's car. Somewhere, coming out of west Texas, early on into the New Mexico desert, I saw him…in the periphery of my awareness, out there in the distance of the desert, but still keeping up with the truck.

***

There was a figure, a man, primitive like a cave drawing, but real and breathing, escorting me into the desert, out here into this new home. He was not with Ruby, he was with me. It's impossible to see things in the desert unless they're really there. It isn't even really seeing as much as it's knowing, it's feeling, it's breathing the things that really are. It's when you truly feel the Spirit that everything becomes perfectly clear.

Me, I guess I was always brought up with a sense of right and wrong. It was always assumed, it never had to be proven, that's just how it was back then. I started to wonder when in my life I'd have to prove what I believed in, to put everything on the line to make myself clear and to make myself understood.

That .380 was catching the heat of the Sun, sitting there on the seat next to me, burning a hole in my soul. I knew it as well as I've ever known anything in my life. Ruby had to die.

***

The pinholes in the night sky pierced through the marbled clouds as I paused and drew a deep breath. Have I really confronted my demons?

***

People, I guess Connecticut Christians, but people in general who say, *"don't sink to their level,"* well those people will also say, *"oh, they'll get theirs!"* as if this asshole who's ruined your life, or robbed you, or beat you up, that someday, *"they will get theirs"* as if someday God will hurl lightning bolts down at the offending party, so you can stand there with your hands clean, deeply reveling in the joy of your enemy's agony, but still be on the road to Heaven.

Someday, maybe *"they will get theirs"* will come from the hands of some less docile adversary, providing justifiable payback for the offensive act. Then, those people can bask in the Christian joy of non-revenge, while another one of God's creatures carries out the Divine Order.

Well I am Karma. I am not afraid and when I feel God's will flowing through my veins, I do not fear my actions that are indeed part of His Divine Payback. How can those Christians, those "children of God, made in his own image," be so afraid that their actions may in some way offend Him? Christians are so afraid to be amassed in the True Nature of God that they deny Primary Experience each and every day of their lives. If they are right in their beliefs, then there will be plenty of time to be passive and benign in Heaven, but Earth is for savoring Primary Experience. Earth is the playground, a serious and Holy playground, but some choose to spend their time in the corner, afraid, and only seeing what actions others will take.

To feel Karma, to feel the energy of God flowing through your veins is the ultimate Primary Experience. To deny the extremes of that flow and the subsequent reactions is to deny the existence of God at all. There are times in this life when God wants you to be pissed off.

THE END

I sat there with my hand on that pistol. Warm and loving she was, not like Ruby. I ran my fingers along the length of its grips, slowly caressing the safety as I went. I slipped the safety off, I don't think anyone in the room heard. It was that easy. I caressed that little love knob and it quivered under my touch. It started pulsating in my pocket as I slowly pulled my anxious fingers away, not wanting her to come too quickly.

She brought me along, that .380…she brought me here, she had the free will, but I never had a conscious thought along the way. I drove all the way up from Albuquerque and it was a long stretch. Lorna Brill, my good friend back in Rigler, told me to make sure I was packing. Fuck that's a long stretch of road out there in that desert, and up into west Texas in the heat of summer with no air conditioning, it was hot as Hell the entire trip. I don't go to the ATM without a pistol, and that long drive alone into the desert made me realize how much I needed that faithful .380 by my side.

As I slowly made my way east of Amarillo, I could taste the air, the moisture. The desert is great, but after living in that dry, dusty air, there's something about the moisture…it just comes on in and picks you up, the lower elevation too. I was starting to get some more oxygen in my brain, started to reel with an awareness I wasn't quite sure exactly when had escaped. You see visions and you hear voices out in that desert, maybe that's part of it, but now I was coming back, coming back down to Earth, now I was seeing the way things really were.

***

Ruby was back in Rigler fucking that brainless hillbilly, Skeeter Pearce, the dumb sonofabitch. I mean in Texas, everyone seemed to be fucking everyone else's mate. There in Texas, another man's wife is the top-shelf champagne...the only skin better is fucking your own, but me, I'm not from that, don't really understand. On the other side of the coin, in Texas, you come home and catch your wife in bed with another man, you can shoot everyone in the whole goddamn house, get an acquittal and maybe a medal, so maybe the risk was the appeal. Maybe in Texas they just wait for that one bullet, a surreal bastardization of "the thrill of being caught"...the fear of discovery, waiting to taste the lead right as the motherfucker comes. Skeeter Pearce? I may be able to help him with that.

I may be able to help him, I may be able to help 'em both, 'cause I'm not really sure what's drawing me there, I'm not really sure what forces are pulling me closer, but closer they pull me...'cause I sure in hell don't wanna be there, an' I sure in hell don't wanna see them, so I'm just following that ol' pistol, in that ol' truck, and I guess I'll wake up when I get there, and see where it is they're all taking me, and why...

***

Ruby was sending me messages, though they weren't verbal. Ruby always liked a good fight, and me, I just wasn't gonna fight with her. I never did give in to her. I guess it's like refusing to fuck a nymphomaniac, but maybe that was the sadist in me. Ruby was saying "hit me!" but I'd smile and tell her she wasn't worth it. It used to piss her off when I'd say, *"Baby, you're just fighting with yourself, turn out the lights when you're through."* I guess in psycho-babble, I was being "Passive-Aggressive", but to me I was just keepin' blood off my hands, and walking away from a whole lot of trouble.

This time though, Ruby may have been getting through. Something I still can't pinpoint exactly what, but something pulled me deeper into Texas, deeper with that loving pistol sending shivers straight to my brain. Something, I don't know what, maybe Destiny...hers, mine, his, fuck I guess Destiny is all the same, but I was heading outa that desert, lower into the plains of north Texas, oxygen swimming into my brain, seeing, finally seeing.

***

I saw Ruby suffer too long in her self-imposed hell. Now I was seeing why none had stayed with her too long, even her family who loved her. How could they? How can you love someone so much and stay so close, and not feel their pain? They had to stay away. Me, I felt so helpless watching her in that place, that place that was so comfortable to her. Ruby reveled in the misery of that place. That place that was so familiar to her...I guess growing up in Connecticut, shit, I don't know if that's what it was, but back there in Leave It To Beaver land, back there I had one flawed view of the human condition, back there I thought there was one common denominator. Back there and for quite some time after that, it followed me...back there I wrongly thought that everyone only wanted to be happy.

Happy, shit...Ruby wasn't the first one. Hell, Tina, Suzi Lo, I can't even count 'em all...they all thrived on sadness and confusion, they all loved their own misery...they didn't want the demons to leave. Me, shit, me the Whiteboy from Connecticut wanted everything to be all right, that's all. I just wanted to show 'em that everything can be cool, that it's okay…that everyone can just be happy.

God, was I naive! I guess in a weird way, I was abusing all those lost souls. I was dangling happiness right there in front of 'em, and showing 'em how things could have been. No one had ever showed 'em how…I was talking a language they could never understand, they recognized the words, but not the meaning, not the emotion. That foreign concept scared 'em so much that they'd lash out like I was hanging food in front of a starving person who'd forgotten how to eat.

All those painful years of watching Ruby suffer in her self-imposed hell, and there was nothing I could do about it. I bought her that .38, perhaps hoping she would have known what was best.

***

There was no way Ruby would've known what was best. Ruby was having a hard enough time just knowing what was. That face in the mirror wasn't always hers, and when you leave yourself, there's not much more you can trust. I gave her that .38, hoping she would know what was best. It was possible though, that she would mistake me for one of the demons, as she often did, but that was a risk I was willing to take.

That late night when I came home and she was sitting up in the bed, back up against the wall, pointing that sonofabitch pistol right at me, I became invisible. I became invisible, just like I used to, being the only glow-in-the-dark back there in east Harlem, back there in Bed-Stuy, corner of Franklin and Monroe, spray-painted there on the wall…"DANGER THIS IS A MUGGING ZONE."

Back there in Brooklyn, becoming invisible so the scared animal wouldn't see me, and wouldn't turn on me in desperation. I had to become invisible, had to fade away, so Ruby, the scared animal could slip back into Ruby.

***

I woke up somewhere east of Amarillo, how far east, I dunno. I drove on through that night, but at that one point, just couldn't keep my eyes open any more. Chain-smoking generics all the way from New Mexico, my head was spinning, and my eyes were just shot from the hot desert Sun.

The sonofabitch truck had a broken pulley, and I left on that late July day, heading out into the eastern desert with no air conditioning, the heat just ate on into me, deeper and deeper, until there was no boundary...I was the desert. I felt the primitives, I was the sand. I got to that point, that one point, where there was nothing else. I got to that one point where all I could say was, *"this is it."* There was no judgment, no right, no wrong, there was just what was.

I have never liked the term "amoral" because although it is supposed to imply the void without morality, it still bases its comparison on the term "moral". The void of morality goes much farther than that. "Moral" is a man-made term that doesn't always mean the same thing. In the Universe, it probably means nothing at all.

You throw yourself into the hands of the Spirit, you have so much faith in the Spirit that you are no longer capable of making the value judgment any more. You leave the man-made morality behind. There is no morality. This is it...this just is.

"God is my Co-Pilot"...how many people really know what that is? How many would really throw away all of their learned Western, Christian guilt, and just ride with God? How many would truly let God lead them, those mortal humans, lead them down that road and to that house. How many would let God open that door for them, not knowing what was on the other side? To me it was more, much more than that catchy phrase on a Christian bumper sticker, that Lincoln Town Car soaring down that long Kansas Interstate.

I was going down that road, I was driving on east, I was going to that place, to open that door…me, throwing my Puritan Connecticut upbringing away, leaving it way back there in that desert. I was gonna allow the Spirit to bring me to that door, to open that door, alone. I was gonna open that door, and go on in and see what was on the other side. There was no turning back. There was no choice.

***

I woke up there, somewhere east of Amarillo, how far east, I don't know. I just rolled on down that state road until my shutting eyes told me that there was no sense kidding myself anymore. It was still dark, but fuck, it was hot and it was humid. I slept with the window open, not knowing where I was, nor who was nearby. At that point, I had already thrown my life to Fate, and Fate was not gonna let some rural thugs get me out there, not that close to my showdown with Ruby.

That humidity was really something. As you leave west Texas behind, heading east, it hits you like some invigorating life force, the oxygen too. It's not better or worse, it's just different, and you feel it deep within you.

I woke up and looked around, but it was still dark. Crickets and bullfrogs made it sound right outa "Tom Sawyer" and I was reminded that I was back in the South. I was no longer in New Mexico. I shook my head and rubbed my eyes. It was a long time 'til sunrise and the dark morning air was cool and invigorating. I still had miles to go. There was no time to waste. Last time I talked to Ruby, she said she'd been living up there in Duncanville, just over the Red River from Rigler, that her and Lizzie were staying with Tracy Rae Clarke, and I had no idea where that was. God was driving me, so I wasn't concerned too much about finding the place, but Ruby, shit Ruby always could throw a slant into things. There was always a surreal hue surrounding her life and everything she touched.

Ruby used to throw a fit and a half anytime anyone would talk about getting high, back in the days...even back there in Rigler, as a teenager growing up, she claimed she was the only one who never even smoked a joint. It was kinda weird, almost like something she had to say to prove to the world, to prove that she was the only sane one, the only honest one, that Ruby was the one who was different, the one who was better. Ruby was the only One.

***

Now me, I hadn't been too carried away with drugs in quite some time. Back there on Ludlow street, there'd be those occasional nights, mostly outa boredom, and then again, there was something about seeing that Lower East Side Sun rising bright outa Brooklyn, seeing the night shadows melt away into the dirty, cracked sidewalk, the ghosts and spirits of many generations of life long gone, slowly slipping away with 'em.

I felt like the only straight back there in the old neighborhood. I went to the gym every day, ate three squares a day, and everything else was just incidental. I finally saw the difference the one day junkies wouldn't sell me valium because I looked too healthy...thought I was a cop. Either way, it didn't matter to Ruby, I had gotten high, maybe I still would, so I was one of them, I was part of the Conspiracy that was keeping Ruby from being what Ruby was really meant to be. It was Ruby against the world and I was no longer on Ruby's side.

Back in Rigler, Ruby was starting to form conclusions from her earlier research into the Conspiracy. Originally it was men who were the assholes, just because God made 'em that way. For the life of me, I couldn't ever ask her what the point was in blaming all the males for all of the world's shit. I told her that if she used the words "black" or "faggot" in the place of "male", her entire argument would not make sense, even to her, but "men" were the assholes, and therefore Ruby could blame all the shit on them. Her arguments were never that logical anyway. It took some time however, but Ruby came to realize that the faggots were also a huge part of the ongoing Conspiracy. After all, it was a male Conspiracy, and gays were male, perhaps the ultimate males, so they were as guilty, probably more guilty than the rest.

***

By the time we hit Rigler, Ruby had figured out that the male Conspiracy was entirely gay. The conspiracy was all about men fucking their daughters and their sons, it didn't really matter which, because it was all about power and it was all about control. Ruby was starting to open up her eyes, the male Conspiracy had a more insidious web of complicity behind it...the faggots were all slowly infiltrating and all the rape and incest and abuse was just their way of cementing their control over everything.

***

So Ruby had this aversion to drugs, any drugs. The night I met her back there in the Cafe on Ludlow Street, back there on that New Year's Eve, the night my life would be immeasurably changed, I was zooming like that's all there was. Ruby had downed about five shots of Southern Comfort before leaving her place, getting the nerve to go out and be among people for a change, to go out there alone, but Ruby's Southern Comfort wasn't drugs, so that was okay.

With Ruby's aversion to drugs it took me a while, it took me a long while, but the longer I stayed with her, the better I saw it. Ruby's demons were her drug of choice. When you're around drug people long enough, you end up seeing that everyone has their drug of choice, their "best friend" drug, all the lesser drugs are sneaking up, trying to take over, competing for control. Ruby's demons were jealous of those other drugs. Those other drugs could have taken control over her, so the demons kept the deepest, the tightest, most insidious control over her. Those demons didn't wanna think that if she flipped for some other ingredients, maybe that would be her road to sanity. Those other drugs would have competed with her demons, and there was too much at stake. Getting high, letting loose, perhaps just stepping back from being Ruby for a brief while was not part of the picture. Ruby had her own reality and as painful and surreal as it was, as paranoid as she had become, that was the reality that Ruby chose to live in. Ruby couldn't be bothered with any other realities.

***

When me an' Ruby were together, I found myself going to the gym less and less, and smoking more and more. Those Camels were the companion Ruby could never be...consistent and available. I found myself liking those Camels more and more as Ruby became less and less available.

Was she unfaithful before she ran off with Skeeter Pearce? I think so, she didn't fuck anyone else while we were first married, but she reveled in her infidelity with her demons. It happened more and more as time went on, but by the end she was thoroughly unfaithful. By then end she just wasn't there anymore. She wasn't there for me, wasn't there for Lizzie, wasn't there for Ruby. I found those Camels were my only friend in those days. Ruby took me away from all my friends, we moved out west, and every time she started to make new friendships, by the next day, she was already working on theories about why they too were part of the Conspiracy that was keepin' her from being all she could be.

On many of those long cigarette smoking walks I'd take, I'd have long, drawn-out conversations with Ruby, who wasn't there. I was all so simple, it was just me an' Ruby talking things over, everything making perfect sense, but I knew it would never happen that way. Logic and reason were not part of Ruby's reality. Conclusions and solutions were not a part of Ruby's tortured life.

Although it could be argued that everyone has their own reality, there were times I wondered if Ruby even had one. Her life was so perilous and inconsistent that sometimes I saw her reality as none at all, it was never the same. Ruby tended to rely on sadness and misery to be her comfort, but even that tormented her. It was so scary and so different all the time, I usually saw her reality as the band of demons pulling the strings, pulling different strings each time, and it was never the same.

***

I'd have these long cigarette smoking walks alone, having all those long talks with only myself, sometimes making me wonder if I was catching Ruby's sickness. I had seen the demons, but refused to let 'em in, so I knew that wasn't it. I started to find that the things that were giving me solace were things that would be considered anti-social or "asocial"...the whole thing began and ended with me and me alone, there was no one else. The entire process didn't involve another living soul, and I wondered if that was how Ruby could have such a surreal place in which she resided. It was incredibly clear and lucid and didn't involve any input or feedback from anyone else. Could there be this much lucidity in this much isolation?

***

I slid my hand off the trigger and let that pistol slide peacefully into the back of my pocket. I left her there safe so she could sleep for a while.

I lit up a cigarette. It was six in the morning and Charlie Bob Clarke opened the door to let me in. Charlie Bob was Ruby's cousin back there in Duncanville, and had been married to Ruby's childhood friend Tracy Rae, but they were divorced now. Divorce just seemed to be a thing people did back there in Texas, a thing they did, perhaps to cement their relationship, 'cause God knows I've met countless Texans who had been married and divorced, remarried and re-divorced, and either were now married to, or living with that very same person again. In Texas it seemed that divorce was like taking a long walk to cool off and in Texas, nothing was over 'til it was over.

Well Ruby told me that she was staying at Tracy Rae's new place up there in Duncanville, but she never told me where it was. When I called her from Albuquerque, she said she'd give me the directions when I called her once I got to Rigler. Ruby had given me a phone number, but once I finally got to Duncanville, I found out that Tracy Rae didn't even have a phone. Somehow I got off the county road and rolled along the Red River, up and down some narrow dirt roads, driving the Rent-a-Truck with car in tow, but I knew I'd find her. I hadn't left that desert to not find her, and after that long drive alone, I was finally seeing and hearing things for the very first time. Except for that brief layover east of Amarillo, I had been on the road for over fifteen hours, and was starting to catch a second wind, or maybe a glimpse of the next life, and I was starting to see right through things and that was really all right.

I finally rolled down that one road where I hit some pavement, and as the Sun was starting to come up, I recognized Tracy Rae's car in the gravel driveway ahead.

***

I pulled into the driveway and tried to turn around, but the fucking trailer was too long, so I swung 'er around and parked down the road under a big cottonwood tree, climbed down from the truck, and walked across the street. I saw no sign of Ruby, and all I did recognize was Tracy Rae's car, so I stopped and stood there for a second.

Now Ruby had just up and split on me, but knowing Ruby, it wouldn't be that easy an explanation. Ruby was back in Rigler, and everything was all right again. There was nothing wrong with Ruby. There were no demons, there was no irrational behavior, there was just poor ol' Ruby, poor Ruby the victim, never done nothing wrong in her life. I started to wonder what it was she had told everyone back there in Rigler, and up north in Duncanville. I knew that whatever she had said, that I was probably gonna be without too many allies. I took a deep breath, reached into my pocket and made sure that that pistol was there, perhaps my only friend at that time. I took my hand outa my pocket and slowly walked on up to the front door.

It was early, the Sun was just coming up, but they knew I was coming that day. I knocked firmly on the door. I waited and knocked again. Charlie Bob peeked through the curtains and opened the door. He motioned me in, rubbing his unshaven face with his right hand. Tracy Rae was still sleeping on the couch under an afghan, and Charlie Bob lay back on the floor where he had been sleeping. I couldn't tell if they were back together or not, but I looked around for clues. There were no beer cans or bottles on the floor and the ashtrays were all full, so I suspected that Charlie Bob was still on his best behavior, trying to get Tracy Rae back. I started to shake a little, and though I wasn't sure, I was starting to wonder if Ruby was even anywhere in the house. I walked over to the kitchen and saw Lizzie sleeping on the pullout bed with Tracy Rae's youngest in her arm. There was laundry strewn all over the floor and I stepped gently as I looked over in the other room.

***

Ruby wasn't there and it was still about six in the morning so I walked back into the living room of that small frame house, and sat in an old worn armchair. Charlie Bob put on a pot of coffee, and fumbled around for a smoke. In Texas and in most of Oklahoma, they never heard of the Surgeon General, and tobacco was the local pastime. Back there, they smoke, snort, chew, dip, and I used to joke that they'd eat it if they could, and later found out that many who chew don't even bother to spit, so I guess they do eat tobacco back there in Texas and Oklahoma. In most of that area, if your trailer was newer than twenty years old, you were pretty well off. They didn't really think of themselves as poor, that's just the way things were. A rich man in Rigler would smoke Camels or Marlboros, but the rest smoked generics, whatever was on sale, the cheaper the better.

I used to cut Broadleaf tobacco back there in Connecticut, when I was a kid, and had probably dabbled with tobacco one way or another for quite some time. I had never gotten hooked, and never really needed it, except on occasions. In Texas however, if you smoked just a pack a day you were pretty much a health freak. I enjoyed an occasional cigarette and I used to have to keep an eye on how much I smoked back there.

Charlie Bob handed me a Basic, which I lit up and smoked deep and hard. I knew now that Ruby wasn't there, and I had to start calming down real fast. An hour later it was just five minutes past six when I was offered another cup of coffee. I lit another Basic off the smoldering butt that I had just taken out of my mouth. It was now six minutes past six in the morning. My heart was racing and I had no place to go, so I started to sit back in that big old armchair and tried to relax.

***

Charlie Bob and Tracy Rae had been married since high school, back when they started making babies together. It's hard to say, but it may have been blissful in its day, and it may have been what Tracy Rae had grown to accept. These are people who may or may not have graduated from high school, but they were in no way stupid. Their wisdom was in other areas, areas peripheral to mainstream American society, perhaps even perverse in some ways, but communicating on their level, they were in no way stupid. They knew what they knew.

Charlie Bob, when orating a tale, like most that could have had other interpretations, would begin with, *"This is the truth the way I see it..."* Charlie Bob was an unemployed truck driver on Disability who dropped out of high school, and had more insight into the subjectivity of things than many of the over-educated scholars and experts who knew that their way of looking at things was the only way people should look at things. Charlie Bob knew everyone saw things differently and that that difference was disseminated from person-to-person-to-person, so to be clear, Charlie Bob would consciously preface a story with *"the truth the way I see it..."*

It's funny that when I left New York and those urban intellectuals gave me so much shit for moving to Texas. Overall, there was a universal intolerance because I was leaving that small slab of concrete in the harbor. I wanted to leave that twenty-mile long collection of concrete, steel and glass, to see what else was out there. There was a pervasive smugness I took for granted until I got to Rigler. There in that town of five thousand people, there were farm boys who had never even left the county, and old timers who had never been out of Texas who with widened eyes and a sense of curiosity, would ask what it was like back there in New York City.

Charlie Bob used to go out and drink dozens and dozens of beers on any given night and drive home, once with the Law stopping him at over one hundred miles per hour. Now Rigler being a small town, usually all they'd do was warn him that they didn't want to go through all the trouble of stopping him again, but watch out when he drank whiskey or moonshine.

***

I hadn't been that close to him or Tracy Rae, all I could go by was the stories, and Lord there were some stories. "The truth the way I see it" was that after Tracy Rae finally left him, Charlie Bob quit drinking. When I stayed at his trailer later on, he chain smoked Basics and drank pot after pot of coffee until well after three in the morning, but never once had a drink of alcohol. Tracy Rae had up and left him, and at least until he got her back, he would remain sober.

The stories develop, they grow, and they change. I don't think Charlie Bob ever hit her either. The only incident I ever found out was true, was the night she sat there much like Ruby, back to the wall, pointing that big ol' .45 at him, perhaps a Texas tradition. Ruby used to say that that was all the evidence she needed, of course Charlie Bob deserved it, he was an asshole. Any woman holding a gun had all the cause in the world, and any man on the other side of the gun, definitely belonged there, and Tracy Rae shoulda just shot the sorry son-of-a-bitch right then and right there. The truth the way Ruby saw it was that there was no man that was ever a victim, but me, I only heard the story of Charley Bob standing there, too scared to move, with his woman pointing a loaded gun at him. That was the truth the way I saw it.

Ruby used to have so many stories about Rigler, and growing to know Ruby as I had, I knew that they had all been embellished with her own special point of view. Overall, her stories were all laced with hints of deception, lies, adultery and thievery, the good ol' boys always taking care of things, and through most of her tales, I saw the thread of evil and deceit that permeated life in that small Texas town. It was a bad novel and a late night movie…way late, like at three in the morning, as you fiddle through the ashtray, looking for one that still has a coupla drags left on it. When we were both living there in Rigler, I had heard so many tales, the truth below the surface. I knew there was a common thread running through 'em all, but I thought that watching all those soap operas had many of those people seeing life through a maze of twisted reality. Television and boredom make good bedfellows, and the thrill and excitement, the necessity for drama were what perpetuated the stories, or so I thought.

***

Ruby had told me things about her father that I never quite knew how to take. Daddy was a ruthless sonofabitch. Daddy came in one night and fucked her as she lay there helpless and young. As far as Ruby was concerned, Daddy had up and fucked all her brothers too, but none of 'em would come forward and back her up, but she knew it had all happened to 'em and they were all just as evil as her father was for keeping quiet.

Ruby always used to say that you should trust your instincts, that those were the voices that would lead you to the truth. She would say that she was psychic, but over time, it seemed to be more paranoia than anything else. She could walk into a strange bar in a strange new town and tell you who the evil ones were and why, and it was always the men. Ruby knew, her instinct told her who the rapists and abusers were. Anyone with a dick was suspect.

I was growing tired of all of her psychic accusations. All of her extreme pronouncement about the evil of men…if she used the word "nigger" or "spic" or any other racial epithet, she would realize what a bigot she really was, but no…Ruby knew the truth and where the evil came from. It was not one or two men, it was all of them. Every single man in the world was an abuser and Ruby's heart bled for all the poor victims, the women and the children, the blacks, that is the black women… never the men, but Ruby grew irate if I ever tried to point out this inconsistency in her Purity. It was men who had fucked up Paradise and it was Ruby's job to interpret all the evil she saw and to listen to her instincts as they spoke to her. Ruby was the only honest one and Ruby's instincts were not to be denied.

The funny thing was, when I would question her about the male Conspiracy, she would usually admit that women too, could be assholes, that everything she detested so much, was human behavior overall. She would try to regroup, and that despondent glaze would take over, as she realized that not even women would help her, that she was the only honest one, the only one, the only one who cared, but she was so outnumbered. Ruby was destined to be the only one, the martyr who cared, but she could only help by being immersed in her own self-pity. Ruby was a Saint.

***

Ruby used to say that she was psychic, but truthfully, she could only see the evil in people. Since she had this gift, she could only conclude that there was no good in the world since she had never been able to find it. Everywhere she went, everyone she met, only reinforced that whatever goodness there had ever been, was now long gone. She blamed drugs, she blamed the Sixties, she blamed Jack Kerouac for bringing us out of our Cold War rigidity.

She lamented about our lost and fallen culture. She revered the Aboriginals and the Native Americans, so far away. Poor Ruby was born in the wrong place at the wrong time, and to the wrong people. There were cultures in which her goodness would be revered and respected. She would be respected for her mystical insights, but in this place, at this time, it was not meant to be and Ruby was alone.

Ruby's father was a hateful sociopathic asshole who only cared for himself. I had never met him, but Ruby used to warn me that if I ever did, that I was to beware. Her father had a Svengali-like control that led people to actually like him, to actually like him despite all the atrocities he had committed, all the lives he had ruined. Ruby would sit, glued to the teevee, watching documentaries about Ted Bundy or John Wayne Gacy, and be amazed at the similarities, and there he was, living under the same roof as she grew up. Ruby was convinced that her father was one of those unconscionable demons who could commit any act without conscience, any act, and still come out clean and smelling like a rose. No, he had never killed anyone, but that didn't matter, Ruby knew he would commit any heinous act without a hint of remorse. To further rub salt in Ruby's wounds, he would cover up all the evil and present himself to the human race and people would actually like him.

I started to wonder why Ruby was the only one who saw her father's evil. Why, if he was such a depraved degenerate, that he left not bodies, but a trail of friends wherever he went. Why was Ruby the only one who could truly see his evil? Was he really Ted Bundy, and if so, why was he not a murderer? Could such a vile sociopath actually avoid consequences as long as he had? Where was his trail of victims? Ruby knew they were out there…

***

Ruby was convinced that there was nothing but a trail of victims, and perhaps her father was responsible for all of the world's victims. At first I believed her, there was no reason not to, but as time went on, it appeared to be such an all-encompassing obsession, the only driving force in Ruby's life, that I began to have my doubts.

Ruby talked about her Aunt Mabel, her father's sister. Mabel Grady was Charlie Bob's mother. Ruby told me about how Mabel got pregnant when she was sixteen. Mabel wouldn't tell anyone who the father was. She went through the pregnancy, more or less with the support of her parents, but would not reveal any details to anyone. When her time came, her brother Joey, Ruby's father, was the one who took her to the hospital. He packed her bags, made her comfortable in his car and they drove off together to the hospital. He slept in the waiting room and didn't leave until she and her child were ready to go home.

***

I sat there on the sofa looking at Tracy Rae and Charlie Bob. It was now about six thirty in the morning, and the Sun had been up for maybe half an hour. My hand shook a little as I took another drag off the cigarette I forgot I had been holding.

Charlie Bob never looked anything like his sister or his brother Tim. I had met their father once, and Tim looked just like him, but Charlie Bob never did. Mabel had died many years before, years before her time, her lungs riddled from smoking too much, and she couldn't breathe any more. I had never met Ruby's father and had only seen photos. He was a big strapping cowboy looking, Irish Texan with curly, reddish blonde hair. Ruby looked more like her mother and her brothers who also resembled her. I sat there across the room from Charlie Bob and noticed his curly reddish blonde hair.

***

Charlie Bob mentioned that they hadn't seen Ruby in well over a week. I looked in at Lizzie sleeping, and realized that she too, didn't know where her mother was. I asked which room Ruby had been staying in and the room grew quiet. Tracy Rae said that Ruby had never lived there...she was across the river, back in Rigler, living at Skeeter Pearce's trailer. I felt my blood swell and lost my breath. My heart started pounding and I couldn't hear the rest of what anyone had to say. I took the burning remains of my cigarette, pulled another one from the pack and kept the fire burning.

I asked if Ruby was even gonna show up today. Tracy Rae said that Ruby said that she was afraid of me and that I was to leave everything there for her and Skeeter. My head started spinning and I reached into my pocket to make sure help was there if I needed it.

She was still there...warm from sitting in my pocket for so long, patient like a good, faithful friend. I rubbed her gently, and she purred like a cat under my touch. Ruby never had a reason to fear me before, but that didn't seem to matter. Ruby's reality was what Ruby made it, and she made it change from day to day. Now I was the one she feared, and knowing Ruby, she probably made that very clear to Skeeter and whoever else would listen. Maybe now was the time I could fulfill her wishes.

What Ruby feared was my calm. I had learned early on with her, to brace myself, to get in a firm, secure stance and stand up to the storm. Hurricane Ruby. I never fought with her, I never fought back, I never argued with her. She wouldn't accept reason if it didn't fit into her grander view of things. Sometimes I would raise my voice, just to be heard. I would calmly point out that her fears and accusations were not based on anything that existed in the physical world. They were fears that helped her feel like the martyred saint, but they weren't real enough to get to her, not real enough to really hurt her. I tried to show her that she was safe, that the demons couldn't really hurt her. I tried to tell her that they couldn't hurt her if she wouldn't let 'em, but Ruby needed her demons, and my calmness irritated her all the more. If I was right about their insignificance, and Ruby could see that, then they would go away and if they went away, Ruby would lose the only certainty she had ever known. I couldn't replace the demons however, I was too stable. Ruby found her security in the instability of her demons.

***

Stability was the abuse I thrust upon poor Ruby. I threatened her with calmness and stability. I challenged her with the notion that life didn't have to be miserable, that she didn't have to wake up to drama every morning. Happiness was not that elusive, but I overlooked one major point. In my attempts to show Ruby that she didn't have to live like a victim, I overlooked the major foundation upon which Ruby based all of her reality, all those thirty-some-odd years. I overlooked the fact that Ruby never wanted to be happy. Ruby wallowed in her own self-pity, and happiness would take away the joy of her misery.

I finally realized that I could offer Ruby the peace that remained so elusive to her. My highly evolved .380 brought me to her. I was never consciously pursuing her back here to Rigler. The Spirit led me, the technology led me, but me, hell…I was just an unconscious animal following ageless instinct. People are all just animals anyway, and I would be vain to think I could make any conscious decision any more than the rest of 'em. Like the animals...people eat, people fuck, and people shit wherever they can. I've not seen too much difference, though the animals don't have the disability of ego and arrogance. The anthills are much larger, and will last somewhat longer, but when the time comes, Nature and the Spirit will wash them all away.

For now, the technology is leading us all to God-knows-where and at this point I realize I have had no choice in any of it. The Spirit led me here in the Divine Order to fulfill Ruby's wishes. I could finally commit the ultimate act of Love. I could now show Ruby she was right. She could be vindicated knowing that she really did have cause to fear me. I could now stop her suffering and put her in that place where she could be happy. Skeeter, fuck Skeeter Pearce...I'm not taking anything from him. He took it from me, and he'll just be the next asshole man who fucked things up for poor Ruby. I will save him from that and save her from him. It was all becoming so clear. I now realized why I came all the way back to Rigler.

***

Tracy Rae had once held a gun at Charlie Bob and Ruby said that was because Charlie Bob was an asshole. All men were assholes, and if Tracy Rae had done something to Charlie Bob, then it was because Charlie Bob had done something worse to her, though we never did find out what that was. Men were always the aggressors and women were angels who were Godlike with the exception of men being in their way.

I had heard horror stories about Charlie Bob, but now that he wasn't drinking, I couldn't tell if he ever was the monster they said he was, but it was Ruby and Tracy Rae, and Ruby had a way of making sure everything came out they way she wanted it to. If Charlie Bob had ever raised his voice to Tracy Rae, then Ruby would have it that Tracy Rae had been beaten badly. Ruby knew as much as she had to about Mabel and Joey, although she didn't come right out and say it except that one time. Ruby had talked only briefly about where she thought Charlie Bob's curly reddish blonde hair came from, and I wondered. Charlie Bob could have had that same sociopathic Svengali trait from years ago when brother and sister secretly coupled, and you had to be Ruby to see through the Svengali, and see the truth, to see everything the way it really was.

***

Ruby used to talk lovingly of her departed grandparents, Rusty and Lil Grady. Back there in New York, when she couldn't wait to get back to Rigler, where things would be okay again, she would talk constantly about how loving and caring they were, but alas, they were gone now and we would visit the gravesite once we got to Rigler.

Before we visited the gravesite, Ruby was full of stories about Rusty, and what a great ol' guy he was, always taking the grandkids out for sweets, and giving 'em pecans from the backyard tree. She told me about him being born in a covered wagon on his folk's way to Rigler, a long, long time ago, and his sweet ol' smile that had lost its teeth, as he got older. After some talk though, she said that they stopped coming by so much as she grew up. Her folks told her that all those sweets weren't really good for her after all, and that they could all visit Papa Rusty at some later time.

When we got to Rigler, not too many people talked about the Gradys. There were some living in trailers on the outskirts of town, and Billy Sue Grady stilled lived in that frame house in town. Ruby stopped talking so much about the Gradys not too long after we arrived in Rigler. She hadn't been back in close to twenty years and things had changed. We went to the overgrown plot where Rusty and Lil had been laid to rest. The stone was cracked and leaning over. The grass that was remaining was overgrown with weeds, but there were more patches of dirt than grass. I told Ruby we could get together and fix up the gravesite, and though she quietly agreed, she never brought up the idea again.

***

I looked across at Charlie Bob, and thought. Tracy Rae had thrown him out over six months ago, but here he was, sitting on her sofa at seven thirty in the morning. In Texas, it seemed that if you didn't stay with your ex, then you never really loved her to begin with. Charlie Bob sure did love Tracy Rae. I couldn't really tell, it seemed to me that if she really didn't want him there, then he wouldn't have been there. It was her house and it was her ex.

Mabel ended up marrying Paul Clark, who took Charlie Bob as his own. Over the years, Mabel and Paul had been married and divorced two or three times. Charlie Bob wasn't even sure if they were still married by the time Mabel passed away. He thought so, but still wasn't too sure. I was starting to wonder if that was what Ruby wanted. Ruby never really thought I loved her, and maybe this was her way of letting me show it...let her go, take her back, let her go, take her back, it would be a love story made in Texas. I suppose I could have taken her back. Hell, she couldn't be too serious about Skeeter Pearce anyway. He was just a bargaining card, an alcoholic on Disability who she could discard when the time was right, when her ongoing prophecy about the evil of men continued to come true. I decided to stay cool, and see what happened next...

***

Ruby used to talk about Paul Clark in endearing terms. Charlie Bob's father was a saint. She told me about how her Aunt Mabel had Charlie Bob without telling anyone who the father was. Ruby assumed that it was her father. She said that Paul's other kids looked more like him and Mabel than Charlie Bob ever did. Ruby figured that Paul Clark knew all the answers but that he loved Mabel too much to judge. Paul Clark loved Mabel Grady and minor details weren't gonna stop that love.

Ruby used to talk about her mother, who her father had kept down for all those years. She said she knew that her mother had been with one other man before she met Joey Grady. Ruby was always proud of the fact that her mother had one up on the old man. While Ruby's father was out fucking all those other women, her mother stayed home, a saint, and Ruby could never forgive her father, nor could her mother ever do anything to even compare with all that he had done.

Charlie Bob talked about Ruby's mom quite a bit. It seemed that he used to see her quite often when he was growing up. I mentioned that Ruby used to say that her mother had only ever been with one other man, and Charlie Bob almost swallowed his cigarette.

His face swelled as he held in his disbelief and he looked over at me, a suppressed look of shock on his face. I thought I had surely missed something. Charlie Bob told me how he knew so much about Ruby and her mother, and why Ruby had so many childhood recollections of Uncle Paul and Charlie Bob and the rest of it all. It seemed that Ruby's mother would bring the kids over to Uncle Paul's house when they were all small and go inside the house with Uncle Paul and a couple of six packs. All the kids would play and such in the backyard for hours at a time, but I guess Ruby was too young to know any different.

***

Charlie Bob told me that Ruby's mom had been with most of the men back there in Rigler, those that would have her. He said that Ruby's father loved that woman to death, but after a while, was tired of wondering when she was gonna come home, so he started going out on his own quite a bit.

Quite simply, Charlie Bob said if it wasn't true, then why did Ruby have so many childhood recollections, recollections of playing out in Uncle Paul's backyard all the time? All of a sudden, a lot of the basis for Ruby's whole view of things started shaking right in front of me. Everyone liked her father, her mother had no friends except a few of the men who still had fond memories, but it was Ruby's father who was the asshole. He was the asshole ever since Ruby was a child. Everything that was fucked up was his fault. Everything that was fucked up in her life was from her father having his way with her, but I started to wonder now if any of that had ever even happened. So far, sitting there that close to Rigler, Texas…things didn't seem to be at all the way Ruby remembered 'em.

***

I looked up and tried to focus on the corner of the wall. I remembered, or thought I remembered that that's where the ceiling met the wall and the walls met each other that there should be a straight line. I couldn't quite remember, but it seemed that there should be a line somewhere in front of where I was looking. I shook my head, closed my eyes, and tried again to focus. The ceiling was flowing like water, flowing down the walls and there were no straight lines. I looked around the room and I realized there were no straight lines anywhere. I looked over toward where Tracy Rae and Charlie Bob had been sitting, but I didn't see them. Tracy Rae had been wearing a pink nightshirt, and a section of the sofa where she had been sitting glowed with a hint of that same pink, but Tracy Rae was nowhere to be seen. I heard breathing and quickly turned around to see who was behind me. The chair I had been sitting in was back to the wall, and I turned around to see the wall swell with life, breathing strong and heavy. I held on firm to the chair, but I couldn't feel it. I grabbed firmly where the armrests had been, but felt my hands sinking deeply into the fabric.

***

If I sit here and look at that lamp, if I pull from deep in my subconscious and the primal urge makes me kick the lamp, break its structure, but leave it functional, so I will live the reminder of my connection with the primitive...will that make me an artist?

"The moment" is not in isolation of the past or the future, but is its fusion...to ignore that is to deny the significance of the moment. To be unconscious of that connection is to defame the beauty of that moment.

I have resented "artists" who feel that a lack of any sort of conscious concern gives them their art. There is a lack of structure inherent in the artistic mind, but reckless abandon only serves the ego and nothing more.

***

Life is always out of control. Those who attempt to have control, typically have the least. There is Divine Payback in the confusion those people find themselves in.

JoLou was a lesbian mother who was in aggression control classes, as a result of the terms of her probation, from what happened in her last relationship. JoLou was so hell-bent on having total control in her life, that all she really had was total confusion. JoLou's life was entirely out of fucking control. Perhaps it was a self-fulfilling prophecy. Without the confusion, there was little for her to control. When people accept the true lack of control, in some way they have more control. There is control over the little things and sometimes those little things add up to paint a larger picture, but accepting powerlessness is the best control anyone can hope for. Things just gust up like a strong wind and hit you in the face, sometimes knocking you down. If you are aware of the possibility of that gust, not knowing when or where, just being aware of the possibility, you are better prepared for the storm.

I think of those middle class Middle Americans who bust into the Walmart in Oklahoma or Indiana, blasting away at everyone in sight. All the neighbors and relatives, all the fellow churchgoers will say, *"he was such a good man, he wasn't the type, I never thought he'd do it!"* If you look at it, of course he was the type, he was the perfect candidate.

Sometimes I think New York is the most stable place to be. Every minute of every day, people are blowing off steam. Granted, they probably have more stress than anyone, anywhere else, but nothing is bottled up. In Middle America, people go to church, get married and live their lives, with nary an indication of discontent. When finally the charade becomes too much, they go way off the deep end. Keeping up the Leave It To Beaver ideals becomes too much for any sentient being. Leave It To Beaver, no matter how seriously you took it, only lasted for thirty minutes at a time.

***

Ruby was always leaving. Ruby had to leave, she had no choice. I could now see it clearly. Ruby's life was thoroughly out of control and there was nothing she or anyone else could do about it. Whether the demons came in uninvited or Ruby had let them in, she was too unsettled to be in one place for very long. There could be no continuity in her life, because if she confronted her past, she would be faced with the hard cold reality of her present. She would have to confront who she was, what she was, and what she wasn't. Ruby would profess sincere connection with truth and honesty, but Ruby was about as twisted and as crooked as they came.

I was first drawn to Ruby because of her pronouncements about how mankind had lost something, and about how we were all doomed from the lack of honesty and sincerity in our troubled evolution. Ruby was honest, the only honest one on Ludlow Street, the only honest one in all of New York, perhaps the last honest person on all of the Earth.

I had never really wanted continuity with anyone and New York was fine for that, but things were changing. I got tired of watching the shadows dancing on the walls. I was tired of three, maybe four in the morning, praying that sleep would soon come. I watched the lines in the ancient plaster revealing faces of the many lives that had lived before me. Things kept on swimming by, and I was starting to feel the need to hang onto something. Then I met Ruby.

Nobody in New York had any real morals. It seemed to me that New York was all about getting away with whatever you could. It seemed like the rip-off capital to me. It seemed like anyone from anywhere, from all across the world, anyone with a scam, ended up in New York, looking for power and money, money and new victims.

I was tired of not wearing sneakers, because no one was really sure if stepping on discarded needles would expose you to the Plague. I was tired of watching them all in line, East Village cool, spoiled white punks from the suburbs who weren't gonna get hooked because they were just experimenting. I was tired of the dope-sniffing children of college professors who would intellectualize about opium use throughout history, and when they finally tried their first needle, they were still "just experimenting". I would go to the bar and unwillingly rub shoulders with all the future famous people, their success always just around the corner. The real successes were in the recording studio or in the gallery actually doing it, not in the bar talking about it. I was seeing right through everything like the sham that it was. I was getting fed up, and then Ruby came into town.

***

I rolled into the Cafe that New Year's Eve half-loaded and dosed for the first time in years. Me, Aussie Bob, and Tia all dropped and went our separate ways. I sat there in the Cafe, disinterested and bored with everything in general. The stuff wasn't as good as it used to be. I didn't know if it was New York, or if times had changed. Maybe I had changed. I mean, it wasn't bad, I was just wondering what else it had been mixed with, what I had really taken.

Ruby walked in, shy and alone. She was beautiful and shining in that green satin cocktail dress she had made herself. Ruby, with her old fashioned dress, with her lovely white face, was a beauty from another time. We danced all night and we talked. Ruby used to talk some talk. Ruby used to talk about all the corruption, and how there used to be a simpler time. Somehow it got to me. At that time, I was so sick of junkies, so sick of all the rip-offs and all the bullshit, that it all made perfect sense to me.

Ruby's past was punctuated with blank spaces and inconstancies. Question marks always arose in Ruby's tales of the past. In a way she had no past. In a way I saw that she didn't want one, and in a way I didn't want her to have one. She told me of her father and the demons, of her stolen childhood. Sometimes people's pasts are too muddy and too desirous of nonexistence. Pasts ring too much of prom dates gone bad, teenage fumbling and the parents who were either too mean, or who wouldn't let you go.

By the time I landed in New York, no one had a past. Everyone was in the present, and you got what you got. To me it was easier that way. There was no baggage, no parents, no longing for glory days gone by. Everyone who made it to that point in their life, and landed in that place, was secure with who they were and parents weren't necessary. In a way, Ruby's estrangement from her family was a relief to me. It was just one tenet of a relationship I didn't have the energy to deal with.

As time revealed, I started to see that Ruby's blank spaces and inconsistencies were actually conscious omissions that helped to keep Ruby in the place she chose at that point in time. Ruby was anything but good, and in place of practicing the goodness and living the honesty she so longed for in this modern time, Ruby found it easier to simply delete sections of her past that proved to be contrary to her pronouncements. With selective memory, Ruby could be the saint, the shining diamond in the night that she so longed to be.

***

Charlie Bob had related how Ruby's father once came roaring back through Rigler, looking for Ruby. I remember the story Ruby had told me about how she had raised Lizzie, and her deaf brother, Ted. This was the first time her folks got divorced, and Ruby and her father moved down to Houston together. She told me about the night when it all became too much, and she had to up and leave for fear of her father. I listened intently and didn't interrupt, as I was not one to pry, especially into Ruby's past.

Ruby and her father set up house, and were living in Houston. Lizzie was a couple of years old and Ted was pretty young himself. Her father worked while Ruby kept the house and watched the kids. From what I could figure out, this went on for close to three years. The way Ruby used to tell it, it was her, and Ted, and Lizzie. Once in a while she'd mention the time when she had to leave her father, but I had to put the pieces of the puzzle together before I realized it all happened at the same time.

Ruby's side of things was that for fear of her father, one night she stole away with Ted, Lizzie, and of course, with her father's shotgun. The way she used to describe her father, I just assumed that the shotgun was a necessary accessory in this exodus, and I never questioned her version of the story.

Charlie Bob, as he saw it, told the story of Ruby's father rolling through Rigler around that same time. Although she told me the horror stories and the extreme sacrifices she made raising Ted and Lizzie, the one thing she failed to mention was the three years she lived with this man she feared so much. She failed to mention that as she was making all those sacrifices, it was her father who had been bringing home the paycheck while she managed the household. Ruby's sainted mother was off running around, so the two of them found this equitable situation. Ruby ran the household so her father could work, and bring home the paycheck, which he put in the joint account. It seems that one day, one day like any other day, he came home from work, and found that Ruby had cleaned him out. All the valuables were gone...his son, his niece, his daughter, and his shotgun were all gone. By the time he got to the bank, he found that the $5,000 savings had been cleaned out, and Ruby was on her way to another blank space in her past.

***

One thing about Ruby...she could never cheat. I knew her better than she knew herself, and that pissed her off more than she could handle. When Lorna Brill told me about that restaurant back in Rigler, I immediately got in touch with Jimmy Scott, and told him I'd put a plan together, and get back to him. The deal was so sweet I couldn't believe it. Jimmy just wanted to recover the cost of the equipment so he wouldn't take too bad a beating.

Jimmy had that little family restaurant back there in Rigler, and had Alice Call running it for him. I met Alice one night at the Hitching Post Bar in Rigler. She was heavy, older and drunk, and so self-assured that not many could stand her for very long. She was loud and argumentative, and I think she mistook all that for foreplay. It was sad and painful to see someone so far gone, without even a hint of a clue. It was hard to believe she could run a business when she was having such a hard time even running her own bar tab.

I never cared much for her and when I found out that the Town Grill was for sale, I jumped on it, but not without some personal inquiry first. It seemed that Alice, who was now pushing fifty, and about a fifth a day, got ditched by her married boyfriend, and went on a royal, Texas-sized bender. Alice never even showed up to open the door of that restaurant for two weeks. Jimmy Scott gave up and realized that it would be best to recoup his loss and not let Alice drag him down any more. The funny thing was that when Alice ran out of money, when Alice ran out of booze, she showed up one day, two weeks later, to open the restaurant. She couldn't figure out why the place had been padlocked and why no one was there.

***

When Lorna called from Rigler, she told me I could get a sweet deal on the Town Grill. Jimmy Scott just wanted to recover his loss and put Alice Call behind him. The deal was sweet, and in a place like Rigler, it was best for a New York Yankee like me to get in with one of the good ol' boys. There was no reason to swim against the stream in a small town in Texas.

***

Ruby was having a tough time at work. Everything would have always been better if Ruby was in charge. Working for idiots just didn't cut it with her. There was always someone standing in the way of Ruby's greatness, someone standing in the way of Ruby doing what was right. There was always someone standing in the way of Ruby saving the world from itself. So now, here in Albuquerque, Ruby was running a store, hiring her own kind, those that would help her save the world, helping those less fortunate, and making sure that everything was run up to her high standards.

Ruby had finally got her own situation, managing a store, a women's clothing store, with no asshole men coming in and trying to ruin things for her. It was hers, and there was no one or no thing that could get in her way now. Well, that lasted about a month, and from that point on, Ruby was miserable again. Nothing was going right, and everyone was getting in her way again. By the time we had been in Albuquerque for just a few weeks, I was wondering how much more Ruby would be able to stand. It seemed to me like all that leaving would take its toll, and there were times I just pictured her spontaneously combusting.

By the time we left Rigler, I had already decided that it was the last time I was gonna leave with Ruby. If it didn't work out in Albuquerque, I wasn't gonna stay with her anymore. In two short years, things had deteriorated into a situation of mutual tolerance, barely.

***

Leaving Rigler seemed to be a good idea at the time, but it was just another escape for Ruby. Ruby felt she was getting away from the assassins who had finally realized that she was the connection to Good, that she was the one who would put a stop to their evil. Although I had never actually seen her do anything to stop their evil, Ruby said that it was her purity, her purity was giving the oppressed their strength, and she knew that the assassins had to stop her.

By the time we hit Tucumcari, Ruby was pissed off again. I don't know how long we had been on the road, but the Rent-a-Truck with my car in tow was a lead sled. When you roll into eastern New Mexico, you don't even notice the climb. New Mexico is "High Desert", and the climb is slow and gradual. Before you know it, you're giving the beast more and more pedal and there's a fuck of a lot of smoke kicking out the back.

We hit the east side of Tucumcari, a point closer to our destination. I slowed down to take in the town. I hadn't been through Tucumcari in about fifteen years, and wanted to check out my surroundings. Ruby had roared up ahead, miles ahead of her demons. She circled around and signaled for me to pull over. Ruby was pissed off again. Why had it taken so long to get there, and why was I driving so damned slow, now that we were there on flat ground? Ruby threw a fit when I told her I wanted to soak in the town on my way through. She started screaming and flailing her arms in the middle of the street, cursing me out in front of Lizzie. I had put up with so much of this shit for so long, it was wearing really thin. Here we were on our way to the next safe place and Ruby was pissed off already. This time, instead of being a calm parent to Ruby, I raised my voice, and told her to shut the fuck up, and to start acting like an adult.

***

I was tired of baby-sitting her and I told Ruby to get a fucking grip. That was it. She ran over toward me in a fur-flyin' frenzy, just about frothing at the mouth. I had been sitting half out of the Rent-a-Truck with the door open, and Ruby, veins bursting with eyes like saucers, slammed the door shut on my leg. That was it. The screaming and childish bullshit in private was one thing. I had seen and I had understood the ghosts and the demons by now, but now Ruby was losing it in public and Ruby attacked me, something I didn't think she'd do, except that one time back in New York. People were looking over, but people were also diverting eye contact, pretending not to watch, but Ruby, don't ever fucking hit me! Pain shot up my leg as I charged out of the truck, just barely reminding myself that I could kill her with one blow. I grabbed her by the shoulders, and shook her, shook her so hard to avoid beating her to death, telling her not to ever fucking hit me again, out there in the middle of Main Street, somewhere in the plains of eastern New Mexico.

I regrouped and stepped back. Ruby was calmer, a distant look of diffused fear in her eyes, but still pissed off. There was no blood, there were no scars, there were no broken bones. I had only handled her until she snapped out of her rage and began to calm down. Ruby then turned to Lizzie and told her that I tried to strangle her and she saw it, didn't she? Of course she did.

"He tried to kill me, and you saw it didn't you, Lizzie? He was strangling me right there in the middle of the street in front of all those people. They weren't going to help, they were all just going to watch but I'm lucky to be alive. He tried to kill me, didn't he Lizzie?"

I knew then and there that the next time Ruby left, I would let her. Life shouldn't be that difficult, especially not when you have an ally to help you through the tough spots. The rest of the trip was a futile and shallow effort, I had finally seen right through the charade. Ruby was stripped naked. She was weak and frightened and her demons were powerless. There we were, halfway to Albuquerque for our new start, and she had already lost it again. She thought she was driving faster than her demons, but they never really left her.

On the way in, out there in the desert, I saw him, walking beside the car, both next to me, and out in the desert, stark and primitive but alongside me the whole way. I'm sure that Ruby didn't see him. Maybe he sped things up. Maybe he knew that Ruby had become baggage, and slowed her down enough for them to catch up with her. Maybe that's why she was so pissed off...she knew they were gonna catch her, alone out in that desert.

***

Ruby's store was near the reservation and Ruby hired mostly Indian women who lived there. They were pleasant and qualified, and Ruby had always held them in esteem from afar. Ruby had always had a deep respect for Aboriginal cultures, particularly the American Indians and the Australian Aboriginals. There were always cultures far away from Ruby that she saw as perfect societies, that she said hadn't fallen from Grace. She saw truth, fairness, and equality at a distance...all the things her demons were keeping her from having in this life. There were people out there who would understand her goodness and appreciate her. They would let her be all she could be.

Ruby's staff were great people, but they were also people. It didn't take long for Ruby to see that there were emotions, anger, sadness, happiness, jealousy, and basic human behavior in these people. It didn't take long, and soon, Ruby was again dismayed that there was no truth left in this world, that there was no goodness. The people she had so much admired from afar had let her down and served to push her closer toward leaving again.

Ruby started screwing things up at work. It was hard work, but a relatively simple job. It didn't take long before Ruby started self-destructing again. Her behavior was becoming more and more erratic and hints of her discovering another conspiracy were brought to her company's attention. There was more evil and deceit at work, and Ruby was gonna fix it, and expose the villains. Before she knew what hit her, the villains found out and dismissed her from her job.

Ruby knew she was cornered. She was on the road to the Truth again, and the long arm of the ever-growing Conspiracy reached out to keep her from saving mankind. At this point, she felt there was nowhere left to go, nothing left to do to save this world. Everything and everyone was corrupt. The evil had even seeped into the desert, it was out there just as strong as it was back there in Rigler. I had seen Ruby on the brink I had seen her demons. Out there in the desert, out there where I had seen the Vision, out there where Ruby had finally left me for the last time, the last time so she could be Pure, I finally saw Ruby completely melt down.

***

I may or may not have seen someone sink that low before. It's hard to tell, but especially without the abuse of substances, without liquor or drugs, it's a far stranger thing to see someone sink that low, to totally lose it, to be gutter-drunk in self-pity. I had seen her sink before, but I could tell that this was it. I could tell, at this point unless she took that .38 and did the right thing, that she was in a pit she would never be able to pull herself out of. I thought that pulling the trigger was probably the best thing for both of us. Me, I was not about to perform that one noble act, that one noble gesture that would have kept me in that place, would have kept me from being in this place now. I was hoping Ruby would know what was best.

***

I looked up and tried to focus on the corner of the wall. I remembered, or thought I remembered that where the ceiling met the wall and the walls met each other that there should be a straight line. I couldn't quite remember, but it seemed that there should be a line somewhere in front of where I was looking. I shook my head, closed my eyes, and tried again to focus. The ceiling was flowing like water, flowing down the walls and there were no straight lines. I looked around the room and I realized there were no straight lines anywhere. I looked over toward where Tracy Rae and Charlie Bob had been sitting, but I didn't see them. Tracy Rae had been wearing a pink nightshirt, and a section of the sofa where she had been sitting glowed with a hint of that same pink, but Tracy Rae was nowhere to be seen. I heard breathing and quickly turned around to see who was behind me. The chair I had been sitting in was back to the wall, and I turned around to see the wall swell with life, breathing strong and heavy. I held firm to the chair, but couldn't feel it. I grabbed firmly where the armrests had been, but felt my hands sinking deeply into the fabric. The pounding got louder and louder, throbbing through my body. I couldn't hear too much else, and I tried to sit back and relax. I sat back, looked up and I saw Ruby standing there, just inside the front door.

***

I looked up and I saw Ruby standing there. She wouldn't look at me or in my direction. She had told me that she and Lizzie had set up housekeeping at Tracy Rae's in Duncanville, but Tracy Rae said she hadn't seen Ruby in weeks. Lizzie had been sleeping in Tracy Rae's spare room, with Tracy Rae's youngest daughter, but Lizzie too, hadn't seen her own mother in over a month. Thinking that they were getting started again, with or without me, I brought a truckload of stuff out of Albuquerque to help them get set up. Shit, if it ain't gonna work, it ain't gonna work, but there was no sense letting Lizzie go without. It wasn't her fault that her mother was so screwed up.

I loaded that entire truck full of stuff, 'cause stuff was anchors anyway. The way Ruby left me alone in the desert like she did, I really didn't' need any anchors, but this was all about finding Ruby and to find out what was really going on back in Texas.

I had been chain-smoking Basics since I got out of the truck three hours earlier. I took a deep drag for strength and looked up at Ruby.

"How have you been?" I asked.

"Why would YOU care?" Ruby scowled back at me.

I stood up and walked in her direction, and she cowered, looking down at the floor and stepping back, like a scared animal.

"DON'T COME NEAR ME!" She screamed.

"Whatever Baby, whatever..." I crooned back at her.

I retreated back to that overstuffed armchair I had been sitting in, and slid my hand into my pocket, back onto that loving .380.

***

I could have ended it right then and there, I could have put Ruby out of her misery. The demons were like virus, they couldn't live without her and if she went, then they would follow. I knew she was melting down, and I just wanted to wish her a fond farewell, wherever it was she was going, but she remained defiant. She was fucking that brainless hillbilly, her own daughter hadn't seen her in over a month, and here she was fucking with me as I was trying to give her a truckload of furniture an' stuff. The world would be a better place, the world would be a better place...

I was amazingly calm although my heartbeat was echoing off the walls and my breathing was strained. It was a lot like Ludlow Street, back in the day, you find a calm center in the middle of all the antagonism. There I was, calm and rational, loaded pistol in my pocket with this raging bitch still antagonizing me.

***

Charlie Bob had some young cowboys over to help unload the truck. When they arrived, we all went out to the Rent-a-Truck to unload everything so I could get me the fuck south to Austin. At this point I had realized that Ruby was beyond repair, and I had to accept the fact that I may not see Lizzie again. It was all over, just like that, and now it was time to move on. At this point, I guess I caught leavin' from Ruby, and now it was my turn.

I was on the truck, doing most of the grunt work with Ruby pissing and moaning about everything. She professed loudly that she didn't need anything from me, and never did, and then proceeded to try to sneak off with my teevee and VCR when I wasn't looking. I just turned down the volume as usual, 'cause it was just a dull roaring buzz I couldn't really hear any more.

Ruby must have sensed my calmness, and as usual that pissed her off. There obviously wasn't enough drama and I tried not to pay attention but the dull roar got louder and louder until I heard her scream…

"THAT DOES IT, I DON'T FEEL SAFE WITH YOU HERE. I'M CALLING SKEETER NOW!"

I had had too many close calls back there in Brooklyn, and on the Lower East Side, this only made me laugh. I knew what had happened. Ruby had told Skeeter that I was violent, probably that I used to beat her. Although I had never met him, I knew Skeeter was one of those gun-toting Texans, and that he was Ruby's latest Superman. He was probably over there, waiting back at his trailer, a pistol in each hand from watchin' too much teevee his whole life, thinking of what she was gonna do to thank him, sitting there waiting on her call. I was not in the mood and this was bullshit, and there's no heroes anyway. That he-man crap never cut it with me before, and was not about to now.

**

I looked up at Ruby with an incredible calmness, unlike any I had ever felt before. I smiled in her face, and told her that it would not be a good idea for Skeeter to come over at this time. My calmness tore through her and her demons flew in front of my eyes as she raged, "THAT DOES IT! I'M CALLING HIM, HE HAS TO BE HERE!!"

I smiled, even calmer than before, and I saw the demons subside, "Ruby...Ruby, Baby, you KNOW that's not a good idea!" and grinned slowly over at her. Suddenly she drew back, frightened, silent.

I turned and walked away from her, back into the truck. The sweat poured down my face in that hot Oklahoma heat. It was humid and hot as fuck and I had had enough. In her one moment of calm, she had seen the Truth, she was aware that there was nothing to her ranting, there was nothing to her conspiracy theories, there was nothing to her threats, and sadly, I no longer believed even a syllable of anything she said. At that point in time there was no Ruby, there was no nothing. I reached into my pocket, slid the safety latch down, turned around and pointed that pistol at her beautiful face, and fucked Ruby one last time.

***

EPILOG

In my mind I have killed Ruby a thousand times, and every time was a mind thrilling orgasm, so full of beauty and light, it drives me from my body. Killing Ruby was the one most noble act to end the suffering of the innocent, to silence the demons, and to tip the scales back to the center.

In reality, or in the brief glimpses of it, it was not my place to fix Ruby's damage. In truth I feel that God brought them together...Skeeter and Ruby. Ruby was damaged white trash, and God took us from New York so Ruby could live in a trailer and I could move on. Skeeter had fucked Ruby a couple of times back in high school, some twenty years earlier, so I am convinced he had no idea what he was in for. Charlie Bob had said that Skeeter was a good ol' boy and that under other circumstances, he and I would have been friends. I told Charlie Bob that I wasn't friends with any man that fucked another man's wife. Skeeter being from Rigler, knew what could have happened. In Texas, sex is the poor man's drug, and another man's wife is the top shelf champagne, but it is also the cheapest way to buy a bullet, especially back there in Rigler.

Since God took her from me, I figured that God could help them kill each other. Ruby left me the week that OJ was on the hot seat. I saw his pained face on the teevee and I knew he did it, there was no question. Maybe seeing him helped me see what would have happened. I don't know, I still feel that Ruby would be better off dead, but as God brought her to Skeeter Pearce, God brought her to Skeeter for him to do the deed. My gift to the both of them was to let those two sorry son-of-bitches just kill the fuck out of each other and make this world a better place.

Then again, Ruby was crazy, stone-cold fucking nuts. Ruby was always dodging the assassins, trying to figure what she had ever done to make the world so jealous of her. Ruby was ever drowning in a sea of confusion, repeating the same mistake after mistake after mistake. Ruby would never learn, and if history is ever a lesson, Ruby is probably leaving again...now it's Ruby leaving Skeeter, Ruby leaving Rigler, and Ruby leaving Texas.

~END~